WINGS FOR NIKIAS

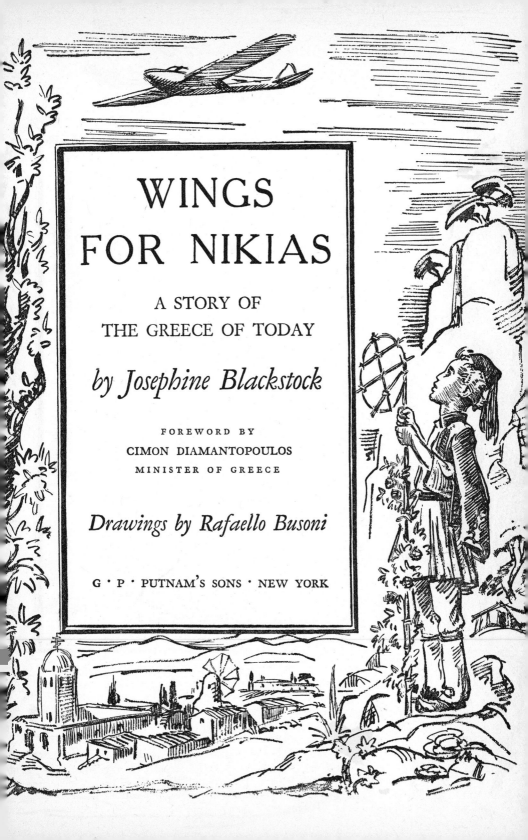

WINGS FOR NIKIAS

A STORY OF
THE GREECE OF TODAY

by Josephine Blackstock

FOREWORD BY
CIMON DIAMANTOPOULOS
MINISTER OF GREECE

Drawings by Rafaello Busoni

G · P · PUTNAM'S SONS · NEW YORK

FOR PERCY BOYNTON

*who first thought that American boys
and girls might like to know Nikias*

FOREWORD

The vitality of modern Greece, the courage of its people, and the progress of the nation are often lost sight of or minimized because of the glorious heritage of ancient Greece. There is much in the Greece of today worthy of the best traditions of the Greece of yesterday; much that shows the persistence and continuity of Hellenic civilization and of the indomitable will and courage of the modern Greeks to carry with honor the burden of that glorious tradition and to revive and, by personal example, to revitalize those principles and ideals which have inspired free people everywhere throughout these many centuries. Any worth-while effort which serves to draw attention to the work of modern Greece, and to instill in the minds and hearts of the children of America, as does Josephine Blackstock's *Wings for Nikias*, a love and wholesome respect and admiration for the enduring virtues of the Greek race, is a welcome addition to the field of choice literature.

> Cimon Diamantopoulos,
> Minister of Greece.

Washington, D.C.

The author wishes to express her thanks to Grace E. Marshall who wrote *Eternal Greece;* Julia D. Dragoumic, *Under Greek Skies;* Harry A. Franck, *I Discover Greece;* and Rennell Rodd, *Customs and Lore of Modern Greece.*

WINGS FOR NIKIAS

Chapter One

AND what happened then?" Nikias asked.

He was a Greek boy. The white linen skirt he wore was called a *fustanella*. Over his shirt was a short jacket, with the sleeves hanging down over his shoulders. On his feet were shoes without any heels, turning up at the toes, with red pompons. On his head was a round cap, called a fez. He had large blue eyes and light hair, and he

13

was rather short for his age, but he could run as fast as a deer.

The young shepherd to whom Nikias was talking laughed and stretched his strong brown arms.

"And then, impatient one," he said, "the king told Perseus: 'There is a terrible monster, called Medusa. She has ringlets of hissing snakes, and—'"

"Why did she have these?" Nikias asked.

"Because she had made one of the goddesses so angry that she had turned Medusa into a monster so dreadful that if anyone so much as looked at her, he was immediately turned into stone."

"What did Perseus do then?"

Demetrios moved closer into the shade of the plane tree. It was only early March, but in Greece then the sun is sometimes very hot at noon.

"Now, hark you, what would you have done? Remember he was but a lad, with no wars behind him."

"I do not know," Nikias said.

"What, is your head stuffed with straw?" Demetrios asked, teasingly. He gave Nikias a poke with his staff. "So you cannot think of a single way to kill a dragon? What is your age, Nikias?"

"On St. Stephen's Day I close my ten years," he said.

"Bah, you grow old," said Demetrios. "Well, then I will have to tell you what Perseus did. He was a brave man, you see, and, besides, the gods had given him two gifts—a great shield and a pair of sandals with wings."

14

"Then he could fly just the way you would in an aero-plano?" Nikias hugged his knees and stared.

"Even so, my Nikias. Medusa was asleep when he crept into her cave. Careful not to look directly at her lest he be turned into stone, he tiptoed closer. In the bright metal of the shield he could see her reflection. He sprang and, with a great lunge, cut off her head."

"And then?" said Nikias.

"He wrapped the head in his scaly cloak and flew away across the sea, never stopping until he came to the land where the sun sleeps." Demetrios jumped up. "Come, there is your tale," he said. "Now let us eat. I have such hunger that I could fall on these olives like a locust on a young leaf."

But Nikias did not stir. He sat there, looking off across the sunny mountain pasture.

"Have the goblins stolen your tongue?" Demetrios asked.

"That Perseus—was very brave," Nikias said slowly.

"So brave that I hear tell there is a temple with great columns built to him in Athens."

"I wish that I could fly," Nikias said. "I wish it more than anything else in the world."

Demetrios threw his shepherd dog a scrap of brown bread. He laughed a great laugh that seemed to come echoing back from the mountain peaks.

"History does not say, my little birdman, where Perseus

left those flying boots," he said. "Otherwise I might borrow them for you."

Nikias did not smile.

"If I could only fly," he said, "in one of those aeroplanos with silver wings I have heard tell about. Have you ever seen one, Demetrios?"

"No. Well, what is to stop you when you have put on a few more years?"

Nikias was looking down at the ground.

"I—am afraid," he said.

"Ho! A Greek afraid!"

"I am not brave like Perseus."

"Do you fear lightning, the fire of God?"

"No."

"Or God's voice in the great winds?"

"No, but—"

"But what, Nikias?"

"Yesterday Theo and I went to the Turks' Cave at the bottom of the black gorge."

"Well?"

"Theo said, 'You're afraid to go inside,' and I said, 'No, I am not.'"

"And of course you were not?" Demetrios asked.

Nikias was looking down again.

"We came to the opening in the cave. It was growing dark, and there was—was something slimy growing on the rock. I remembered what Papous said, that the Turks used

16

to torture their Greek prisoners in there, and I—I turned around and ran straight back home."

"There are not any Turks in Greece now," Demetrios said, laughing. "All that happened a hundred years ago."

"But folks say a wicked goblin still walks at night near the cave," Nikias said.

"Did you ever see him?" asked Demetrios.

"No." Nikias hung his head. "Demetrios, Theo—he said I was a coward. He said he was ashamed of me."

"Ho, the shoemaker's son gives himself airs." Demetrios sniffed. "I would not let that worry me." He leaned over and patted Nikias' arm. "Come, little solemn face, I will play you the shepherd's song on my reed, and then you must be starting down the mountain, or Kyra Yannio, your grandmother, will worry."

Demetrios finished the last piece of bread and cheese, then lay on his back and began to play on his reed.

He was a tall young man, with dark matted hair and clear gray eyes. Nikias loved him. He knew that Demetrios could see farther than anyone in the village because he was used to watching his sheep and goats. He knew that Demetrios could give a queer call that would bring the goats to him from as far as half a mile away. He thought that the stories Demetrios told were the most wonderful in the world. But the reason Nikias loved him most was because he was always laughing, happy, and never sick. Sometimes Nikias wondered if this was because Demetrios stayed most of the time in such a beautiful place. There were great rocks every-

17

where; the tall mountain peaks reached right to the clouds. There were thin, dark cypress trees, just opening, and bright holly and oaks. The shoots of the buttercups and anemones were just beginning to show.

Demetrios was very poor. His house was a blanket stretched over crossed sticks; his furniture, a few caldrons and pails and cheese pans. But Nikias thought Demetrios had a wonderful life. Sometimes Nikias was allowed to sleep all night there, and then Demetrios would get out his reed and play to him, or tell him stories. Demetrios knew all about the great myths and tales of Greece that go back thousands of years, and Nikias would lie, hardly moving, listening to the stories. Sometimes, very late, they could hear the nightingale sing, and smell the pine needles, and before he went to sleep Demetrios would whisper to him about a place where he could find a blackbird's nest.

But now the time was over, and Nikias got slowly to his feet.

"Will you come back with me?" he asked.

"Oh, ho, if I only could!"

"You could see Thalia," Nikias coaxed.

Demetrios was going to marry Thalia soon, Nikias knew. Penelope, Nikias' little sister, was counting the days until the wedding, she wanted so much to dance and sing and eat sweetmeats at the wedding feast. But Nikias was not so sure about that marriage; he was afraid Demetrios would not find any more time to tell stories or play on his reed.

"You know I cannot come today," Demetrios said.

Nikias sighed. "Then good-by," he said.

"The good hour be with you, little one," Demetrios answered. "Come soon again."

"Perhaps on Tuesday?" Nikias asked eagerly.

"No, Tuesday is unlucky; another day."

Nikias started down the rocky slope. As he went, he could hear Demetrios' happy voice singing this song:

> "Of all the stars in heaven,
>   But one is like to thee;
>   The star that comes at midnight,
>   And makes the others flee."

Nikias knew Demetrios was thinking of Thalia. He thought the song was rather silly, and shrugged his shoulders. Nikias walked fast. Presently he came to the terraced lower slopes where the vineyards and olive trees grew. He looked at the small silver-gray leaves of the olives and thought that soon the fruit would be ripe; then the cherries and the big cucumbers would come.

Presently he grew thirsty and stopped beside a little clear stream. Its waters were mineral, and so Nikias knew that the stream was protected by the Nereids. Didn't all the children in the village believe this was so? The Nereids were nymphs, and the only way to get the best of them was to snatch at their tunics and keep the torn piece always with you. But since Nikias had never seen a Nereid, he had not been able to do it so far. He knelt and drank the cold sparkling water through a folded leaf. Then he went skipping along again.

He felt very happy now. He had forgotten all about Theo and the Turks' Cave. What fun everything was! Even to touch these stones, worn so ripe and smooth, made you feel good inside. And right here was that olive tree that Papous, his grandfather, said was more than two thousand years old! Why, it must have been growing when Greece was the greatest and wisest country in all the world. Ho, he wished Demetrios could see those white clouds right over his head; they looked just like sky sheep. Nikias' feet began to dance a little jig. Soon it would be Easter, and then there would be great doings. He and Theo and Penelope and the other village children would put a queer, rudely carved head of a bird on a round wooden stick, and carry it through the streets, singing a song about how the swallows had come and about the gifts they had brought. People would come to their doors and give them little presents. Later on there would be Masquerade Day, and hadn't he a special secret about it!

Then Nikias came to a gorge where the trail was so narrow that the four feet of a mule could hardly have trod it safely. Down below was a drop of fifty feet. Nikias shivered, looking down into the black depths. Then he thought of something Manitza, his grandmother, had said to him yesterday: "When your body trembles, make it still by looking up at the heavens."

So Nikias looked up, and there, soaring high in the blue

sky, he saw an eagle with its wings stretched out. It looked just like the picture that his teacher, Kyr Mihale, had shown him, the one of the silver aeroplano. Nikias' heart began to beat very fast. He thought how much he would like to ride in one of those planos, to pilot it himself; but how frightened he would be.

"I can never do that," Nikias said to himself; "I'll never have enough courage."

And he began to run very fast down the trail toward home.

Chapter Two

WHEN Nikias came to the village, he slowed down. He began to feel very ashamed of himself. Around him were all the things he knew and loved, and he felt safe again. There was the little white village, with the red roofs; the gardens where later on would grow the delicious vegetables, cucumbers, endives, and artichokes. There was the thorny plant that grew over the fences to keep the goats and chickens out. He passed the well where the women drew water in great clay pots. He came to the little church, and the market place with the wooden booths where fairs were held. High on the hill he could see the Miller's big blue-washed house with the balcony and the vine-covered porch.

Then Nikias was running up the little, worn path to his home, past the loom, the kneading trough, and the beehive-shaped oven where Manitza set the bread to bake. The house was built of stone, and was just one story high, with no windowpanes, only painted shutters, but Nikias was sure it was the finest house in all Greece.

He opened the door, sniffing happily. He could smell the greens cooking; he could even get a whiff from the strings of onions, and the dried herbs and fruit hanging from the rafters. Yes, it was a pretty fine house. Had it not a real table; while Theo had to sit on the floor when he ate! Had it not straw chairs and a big cupboard to hold dishes and cooking pots! There was the wooden rail holding the stack of rugs, mattresses, and blankets in which he and Penelope curled so cozily at night. Manitza herself stuffed the mattresses with maize husks and covered them with carpet stuff. You never felt cold on that mattress when you slept outdoors under the plane tree. Manitza saw to that, but then did not Manitza see to everything! In all the years, she had never once let the two oil lamps on the mantel go out, or the little light burning under the eikon picture of the Virgin Mary.

"Manitza, here I am," Nikias called.

Manitza was stooping over the grate fire, stirring the pot of greens. Penelope was sitting on the floor beside her. At the sound of Nikias' voice, Manitza turned around. She was a tiny person with a wrinkled brown face.

"You are late, my Nikias," she said. "The shadows grow long."

"Don't you see supper is ready?" asked Penelope.

She was a pretty little girl with blonde hair and laughing brown eyes that looked hardly darker than her tanned face. She wore a short, wide jacket with wide sleeves, a white skirt, an embroidered apron, and she had a bright yellow kerchief tied about her head.

"Why were you so late, little one? Did you find a rabbit's nest?"

It was Papous speaking. He was just coming in at the

23

door, a strong old man, with kind blue eyes. Over his *fu-stanella* he wore a long white coat. He held a clay pipe in his hand.

"No," said Nikias. "Demetrios told me a story, and played on his reed."

"Ho, and what tales of the heroes of Greece did he tell you this time?" Papous asked.

"It was about Perseus and his sandals with the wings, and the way he killed the Gorgon."

"How your eyes shine!" Papous said. He laughed. "Now you, too, will slay a Gorgon, I suppose?"

"No," Nikias said. "Papous, I would like best to fly like Perseus; only it would be in a great silver aeroplano with engines that talk very loud."

"Oh, ho, silly one," Penelope said; "you would never have the courage."

Manitza was setting the greens on the table in a casserole. She turned and looked at Nikias.

"I have seen even a small bird very brave," she said. Then she smiled. "Come, draw up your stools. Penelope, you have helped me well, so you shall have roast figs for a treat."

They sat down around the table that was set cozily close to the fire, for the evenings had turned chilly. The greens, cooked in olive oil, were set in the center of the table. That was all there was to eat except cheese and olives and delicious brown bread.

"I have news for you," Papous said, after a minute. "I

met the postman just as his donkey was turning into the square; he had a letter for me. Kyr Mihale was there so I asked him to read it to me."

Manitza gave a little cry.

"It was from Vasilios?" she asked.

"Papous, tell us, tell us!" Nikias said, his eyes wide and shining.

"The letter would not interest you," Papous said teasingly; "it is just about someone who will make a long trip."

"Oh, oh!" cried Penelope. "It's our uncle Vasilios! He's coming from America to see us!"

"The letter was from Vasilios," Papous said, "but it is of his son, Paolos, that he writes. He will send him here for a visit."

"May the Virgin be praised," Manitza said with a sob. "Now I shall see my son's son before I die."

"Papous, Papous," Nikias shouted, "is he a lad of my own age?"

In his excitement, Nikias had forgotten even to eat.

"Will he play bronze fly with me?" asked Penelope.

"And hunt for blackbirds' nests in the hills?" shouted Nikias.

Papous smiled. "Paolos has already closed his twenty-first year," he said.

"Oh, he is old," said Penelope, sighing.

"Perhaps—perhaps he will tell us stories like Demetrios," Nikias said, but his face had fallen, too.

26

"It is possible," Papous said. "Vasilios writes that he is a birdman."

Nikias' spoon fell with a clatter. He stared, his mouth open, his eyes round.

"He can fly an aeroplano?" he asked in a whisper.

But then everyone began to speak at the same time, Penelope, Manitza, Papous—exclaiming, wondering when Paolos would arrive; what he would look like; whether he would be American or part Greek; whether he would tell them all about the great city of New York. Nikias' question stayed unanswered.

After a while it was quite dark. They could hear someone playing a fiddle down the street, and the birds were cheeping sleepily, and everyone went to bed. But Nikias lay for a long time with his eyes wide open in the dark. He was wondering about this new cousin of his who could fly a great aeroplano high in the sky. Would—would he teach Nikias how to pilot one? Would they climb high, high into the great blue sky, with the white clouds running before them? Would they race faster even than the wind? Nikias gave his head a little shake, and sighed. What a foolish one he was! Hadn't Papous said that an aeroplano cost as much money as a palace in Athens? Well, then, he and Paolos could *talk* about the ships. Oh, when would he come? When would he come? And how could he, Nikias, show him welcome? Would Paolos like Demetrios, and the hills, and the games Theo and he played, and the sound of the nightingale late at night? Americans were great people,

27

with much money, and big buildings that touched the clouds. What would Paolos think of the village and Kyr Mihale and Masquerade Day? Well, anyway, he would like Papous' house, for was there not good luck here? Had not the swallows once more built their mud nests in a corner of the rafter this spring?

Nikias fell asleep.

Chapter Three

THE next day Penelope was sitting in a corner of the schoolyard. Lessons were over and she was playing with her special pet, a great dried old beetle dressed in a tiny kerchief and lying in a cradle that Papous had carved out of a walnut shell. She was singing a song that Kyr Mihale had taught them. It went:

"Moon, bright moon, so full,
Shine now as I go to school,
To learn to 'broider and to sew,
And all the will of God to know."

That was funny, Penelope thought; Kyr Mihale's grandmother had sung that song a hundred years ago when she was a little girl, and lived on an island called Andros. Then the Turks did not even let Greek children go to school. Well, she, Penelope, for one wished some Turks were here now so *she* would not have to go to school. Spelling and reading and counting were just a waste of time when all you wanted was to talk about weddings with Thalia. But Manitza had said today that Thalia was so busy Penelope must not pay a visit to her.

Penelope broke off her song, and sighed. What was the use of spending every Saturday afternoon at church learning the liturgy and the Easter songs, going to sleep every single day last summer at noon so the nymph that walked in the heat of the day would not punish her, planting and weeding the garden Kyr Mihale had dug for her—all if she could not talk to Thalia about that wedding? After all, she was going to be one of Thalia's bridesmaids, was she not? Thalia must have seen she was pretty nearly grown up when she had asked her.

"Penelope! Penelope!"

She looked up. There was Nikias racing toward her, his bare feet kicking up little puffs of dust.

"I have been looking for you everywhere," he said.

"What is it?" Penelope said.

"Thalia has sent for you."

"For *me*?" Penelope's eyes were shining; her cheeks looked like two dark roses.

"Yes."

"Did she tell you why?" Penelope asked. She was stuffing her beetle into the bright woolen bag she carried.

"She said she was going to make you a costume for Masquerade Day."

"Nikias, she said *that*? What else, Nikias, what else did she say?"

But Nikias did not answer. His toe was digging into the ground; he was not looking at his sister.

"What is the matter? Why don't you say something?" Penelope asked.

"Penelope," Nikias said slowly, "will you ask Thalia whether she will tell me how I can look the way Perseus did?"

Penelope stared at Nikias, her mouth hanging open.

"He who wore the wings on his sandals?"

"Yes."

"But why should you wish to look like him? He was a great hero."

"Do we not all go clad as someone on Masquerade Day?" Nikias said in a sort of angry voice, because he was afraid Penelope might laugh. "Tell her that I will bring her holly branches and fagots for a whole week if she will be so kind."

"I don't think she will find time for the affairs of a mere boy," Penelope said importantly. "She—she probably wishes to ask me what color embroidery to put on her jacket. She knows that I am a *very* good embroiderer."

"Penelope," Nikias said in a low voice, "if you will ask her, I will give you one of my red Easter eggs—no, I will give you *two*."

"You will?"

"And I will gather you a bunch of iris for your hair," Nikias said, his voice hoarse he was so anxious.

"It is a bargain," Penelope said, well pleased at the way things had turned out. Then she laughed merrily and said, "Oh, ho, I would have asked her anyway."

31

Penelope picked up her bag and ran skipping out of the playground and down the street.

Nikias followed her slowly. He was thinking of Perseus, and how he, Nikias, would dress for the Masquerade like the picture Kyr Mihale had shown him today. Would Demetrios be able to see him? And might there just be a tiny chance that Paolos would arrive sooner than the letter said?

Near the bamboo fence Theo was sitting, tossing up knuckles for jackstones.

"Can I play?" Nikias said.

Theo was a tall strong boy, a year older than Nikias. He could throw a dart farther than any other boy in school, and could wrestle and jump.

"No," Theo said. He did not even look up.

"I will be 'it' and let you hit me first with the whip if we play bronze fly," Nikias said.

"Smarty!" Theo sniffed loudly. "Do you think you can get me to play *that* way?"

"What do you mean?"

"Ho, you are all right for hide-and-go-seek or cleaning off the blackboard," Theo said. He thumped his chest. "I might even let you play ninepins with the empty shells the Miller brought back from his hunt, but what I am looking for is someone with a stiff enough backbone to go into the Turks' Cave with me after dark."

"The reason I was scared the other day," Nikias said,

32

not looking at Theo, "was because I—I saw a Turk peeking out of the cave."

"Pooh, you are always getting frightened over the silly things you see in your thoughts," Theo answered. "On your way and play lady bugs with Penelope!"

Nikias did not say any more. He went out through the gate and along the path, passing the big stone the children used as a shadow clock to tell the time. He stood still. Why, it must be close to half past five, the shadows were so long! He would have to hurry or he would not catch Papous before he started home. Manitza had told him to go to the coffee shop and tell Papous to be sure to bring back a bag of salt.

"Do not hurry him," Manitza had said. "That smoky old place Papous loves next best to home. He would rather talk about the affairs of the world there with Kyr Mihale, the Miller, and the travelers, than he would eat his food. Well, it puts new blood into his veins; I do not grudge him the time. But look, Nikias, be sure that you catch him before he starts for home, and tell him about the salt. Else I cannot make the lamb soup."

Nikias hurried along the street. It was later than he had thought. The coffee shop lay a stone's throw from the church and the Pappas' house. Nikias unlatched the door and slipped quickly in. Papous was still there; so was Kyr Mihale. But they did not notice Nikias; their backs were turned to the door, and they were listening to a stranger talking. He was a big, broad-shouldered man who wore Eu-

34

ropean clothes. Nikias gave his head a little shake; the coffee shop looked different. There were the same smells of tobacco, spices, Turkish coffee, and burning holly logs; the blackboard with the names of the people who owed money; but it was not the same. Perhaps it was because, except for the stranger's voice, there was not a sound in the room.

Nikias felt a little prickle of excitement. He stood with his back pressed against the wall, listening. The stranger was leaning toward Papous, a glass of wine in his hand, his eyes very bright.

"Bah, the enemy will see to that! One of these days some soldier will be found mysteriously slain just across our borders, and the price for forgiveness will be this province or that. There will be war as sure as the sun gets up in the east, unless—" The stranger spat into the fire—"unless Greece has sense enough to give the enemy what they want."

There was a little silence, and then Nikias heard Papous say:

"Give me your name, master."

"Patras—from Athens," said the stranger. "I travel for a tobacco house."

Nikias saw Papous lean toward the man.

"You mean that you do not wish Greece to defend her own country?"

The man drank deeply of his wine; he laughed a loud laugh.

"Am I a hero, that I should advise our country to throw itself over a precipice, grandfather?"

"Greeks are free men," Kyr Mihale said in a stern voice. He was sitting near Papous. "And their country is dear to them."

The stranger shrugged.

"I would rather be alive than dead," he said.

The old man, the owner of the coffee shop, spoke in a whisper:

"When do they say this war will come?"

"Who knows? Perhaps this summer, perhaps this fall. Well, time flies; I must be on my way." He picked up his hat, threw a coin on the counter, and turned toward the door. Then he saw Nikias standing there.

"Oh, ho, so this little cockerel has been listening," he said. "Who may you be, boy?"

Papous and Kyr Mihale turned around quickly.

"He is the child of my youngest son, who, with his wife, died of the fever," Papous said.

"He is a fine child, grandfather," the stranger said. "May he live to you."

Nikias stood there staring at the stranger.

"Master," he said, "will there be a war in our land?"

The man spat on the floor.

"So the cockerel sticks his beak into the affairs of his elders," he said. "Have they not told you that you will eat sticks if you do that?" He turned the handle of the door, lifted his hand and gave a second loud laugh. Then he was gone.

No one said anything. Outside Nikias could hear the

sound of the stranger's footsteps. Then he heard rain falling.

"God has let loose the goatskin," the owner of the coffee shop said. "It is raining."

Why were Papous and Kyr Mihale looking so sad, Nikias wondered. War was when soldiers shot off their guns. If there was a war Theo and he would have many shells to play with. But no one would make war on Greece. How could they? Greece belonged to Papous, Manitza, Penelope, Demetrios—all of them.

After a minute Papous said, "Come, my Nikias, we must go home to supper."

And they went. Nikias had forgotten all about the salt.

Chapter Four

THE day after Nikias went to the coffee shop, he and Theo were walking down the mountain trail toward the village. It was a fine sunshiny day. The sky was as blue as Papous' eyes, the sun as gold as the coins that Thalia wore about her head of a Sunday. Kyr Mihale had taken his pupils for a walk up the high slopes. He had shown them queer-shaped rocks, and had pointed out an oriole's nest and a clump of early iris. Nikias in turn had found a young wild pear tree, and they had all sat under it and eaten their sandwiches.

"I wish that school was always like this," Theo was saying.

Nikias shook his head, which in Greece means yes.

"With birds and butterflies instead of books," he said.

He was glad Theo was talking to him again; perhaps he had forgotten all about the Turks' Cave.

"What a blow that was the woodcutter gave that big oak back there!" Theo said. "The sound was loud enough to kill a demon."

"But yet I like books, too," Nikias said slowly, "because there are stories in them."

"Bah," said Theo. "You and that old bookworm, Kyr Mihale!" Theo gave a shout. "What a joke that was on Penelope when we played blindman's buff and I jumped out from behind Kyr Mihale and frightened her near to death." Theo threw back his head and laughed very loudly; like all Greek people, he loved to play tricks. "Oh, ho, I wish Lent was not so close, when we cannot eat what we will, nor laugh and play games."

"Well, last week was meat week," Nikias said. "That was fun. The butcher killed a pig for every family in the village, Papous said. Oh, but that pork was juicy! Manitza said we hardly left enough of it to salt down and smoke."

"And this is cheese week, with the Masquerade on day after tomorrow," Theo said. "I suppose old Kyr Mihale will hold our noses in our geography books right up to the very minute the parade starts." Theo blew out his lips. "That old school," he said; "reading and writing from nine until noon; history and arithmetic from two until five. Why didn't Kyr Mihale stay in his Island of Andros? *I* do not need his old lesson books."

"Kyr Mihale says it will be useful to know this learning when we are grown up," Nikias said. "Manitza says she did not even have a school to go to; she sat with the other children in a circle under the fig tree, with the teacher in the middle telling them about Aesop's Fables. Papous, he has never even learned to read or write."

"When I am grown," Theo said, "I shall make a law that no boy will have to go to school for four whole years. There will be a policeman to shoot him if he does."

"If only we could have climbed all the way to Demetrios' place!" Nikias said. "*He* can teach you more than all the schools in the world."

"Bah, *I* know what you want there," Theo cried. "You would fill your ears with more tales about the great Perseus." Theo slashed at an osier bush with his stick. "Nikias and his god! They are like Kyr Mihale and his lesson books."

"Theo," Nikias said in a low voice.

"Move away a bit," Theo said teasingly; "those wings on your sandals tickle my ankle."

"I shall go to the Masquerade the day after tomorrow in the dress of Perseus," Nikias said. "Thalia promised to make me the tunic and mask."

"Bah, you are crazy!" Theo shouted. "Tell me, how can you make the flying sandals?"

Nikias' eyes were shining. "Manitza bade me find the wings of two turkeys. This I did, and she put little splints to hold the feathers apart; then she sewed them to an old pair of sandals."

"That is nothing," said Theo, trying hard not to look envious. "*I* shall go as a huntsman, with a great knife in my belt, and perhaps even some gunpowder."

"Come home with me, and I will show you my wings," Nikias said. "Manitza perhaps will let you stay to supper."

"Maybe I will take a look at those sandals if I find nothing better to do," Theo said in a very lordly voice. But his black eyes gleamed; there was nothing Theo liked better than Manitza's *trahana,* with its wheat and milk and nuts. "Come, I'll race you there."

But on their way the two boys decided to stop and see the Miller's new donkey, so that when they reached home, Penelope was already there. She was slowly and carefully embroidering a flower on some cloth.

"What brings you children home so early?" asked Manitza. "The shadow clock says it is not yet five."

"Kyr Mihale took us for an excursion into the mountains," Nikias said. "Didn't Penelope tell you?"

Manitza made a clucking sound with her tongue, and smiled.

"That little vain one," she said, "remembers nothing

but the new jacket she will wear to Thalia's wedding. Now she makes a silver flower."

Manitza was cleaning the oil jar with a cloth, for water is scarce in Greece and one never wastes it.

Theo gave a little jerk at the twisted thread of red and gold tied around Penelope's wrist.

"Are you trying to embroider your *hand?*" he asked.

"If you have a daughter dear to you, do not let the March wind see her," Manitza said. "The thread will keep the sun from darkening her skin. Tell me, did you see any blue lupine in the hills, Nikias?"

But Nikias was not listening. High up on the rafters, he had caught sight of a pair of sandals, with wings—wings that were dyed a shining silver color.

"Manitza, Manitza, my Perseus sandals!" he cried. "Get them down for me, please."

Manitza smiled and, standing on a stool, took down the shoes and handed them to Nikias. His hands, she saw, shook so he could hardly hold them.

"You must have a care, my little Perseus," Manitza said, gently, "or one of these days *you* will be flying away to fight another Atlas."

"Perseus fought the *Gorgon,* Manitza," Nikias said.

"And the great Atlas, too," Manitza said. She was opening the chest and taking out the earthenware jar that held the *trahana.*

"Tell us, Manitza," begged Nikias.

"But I shall be stealing Demetrios' thunder," Manitza

43

said, smiling. "Well, the story goes that Perseus, weary with his journey, sought rest in Atlas' country. He was the king, and a mighty man, bigger than any giant."

"Didn't he welcome Perseus?" asked Nikias.

"At first, and then he remembered that he had been told that one day a young warrior would do him harm. So he bade him be gone, and when Perseus refused, he lunged at him with his sword. But Perseus saw that Atlas was too great a man for him to fight, so he said to him: 'Let my enemy aid me now.'"

"What did he mean?" Theo said.

"He meant the Gorgon's head; for saying this, he turned it full in the face of Atlas, and—"

"And he became stone?" Penelope asked.

"That he did. They say his head and arms and legs grew bigger and bigger, and became stone mountains and valleys and seas. That is why Atlas still holds up on his shoulders today the whole world."

Nikias did not say anything.

"You listen with your ears, but you do not hear," Manitza said, looking at him.

"I was thinking what a great life Perseus must have had, flying with those sandals, fighting the Gorgon."

"Well, but you will be wearing Perseus' sandals," Penelope said. She laughed. "Even if they really are our old turkey's feathers."

"*I* should be the one to wear those shoes," Theo shouted. "I am never scared of anything, even a brigand."

44

"Come, now, my little ones," Manitza said; "see the fresh loaf of bread I have set for your supper."

"Oh, you are always talking big, Theo," said Penelope. She was folding up her work. "Manitza, may I toast a slice on the spit?"

"Bad luck comes to the crops if one toasts bread between sowing and reaping time," Manitza said.

"Will Paolos know that I am Perseus?" asked Nikias.

And then the others all laughed very loud, for Nikias had forgotten that Paolos would not be there for many a week.

"Wake up, dreamer," scolded Manitza. "Come, set stools about the table, and take your fill. For the forty days of Lent, you will not have meat or butter, eggs or cheese. Best make the most of things now."

But when Nikias sat down, he still held on his lap the silver sandals.

Chapter Five

THALIA sat under the olive tree in front of her cottage and sewed on the Perseus tunic. Penelope, her pretty curly head pressed close, leaned against Thalia's shoulder.

"If you would only stop sewing, and talk to me," Penelope said.

"Lazy one," Thalia answered, smiling, "tomorrow is Masquerade Day. Do you not wish Nikias' costume to be ready?"

"That Nikias! All he talks about the whole day long is flying. Now Demetrios is carving him a tiny aeroplano out of cherry wood."

"And does it fly?"

"How could it, a toy?" Penelope said, pouting because Thalia was not treating her like a grown person who knew all about embroidery and ribbons.

"Nikias' thoughts are always flying somewhere," Thalia said; " 'tis a wonder they do not carry him off the way the winged sandals did Perseus."

"It is all very silly to talk about aeroplanos," Penelope said. "To stay on the earth is best."

"It must be very wonderful to fly, Penelope."

Penelope twisted a corner of Thalia's apron; she wasn't listening.

"Nikias says when you marry Demetrios he will have no more time to tell stories," she said.

Thalia laughed. "That silly one! I shall leave them alone often; men like to talk about their own affairs."

"And we like to talk about *ours*," said Penelope. "Thalia, do you think I will grow up to be beautiful, and wear velvet clothes with gold and red embroidery and fine laces?"

"A young maid should not have such vain thoughts," Thalia said. "She must turn her mind to being kind and wise. She must learn to lift and fold and handle things so

47

that whatever she touches will be the better. That is what my mother tells me."

"When I am a grown woman, I shall marry an American," Penelope said, "and he will buy me necklaces and rings and fine aprons, and I shall live in a great house in that place called New York, with a real rocking chair, and wear a velvet mantilla all day long—even when I go to bed."

"Ah, an American rocking chair," Thalia said with a little sigh, "I, too, would like that. Well, my little one, you must ask this cousin Paolos of yours to build you the house."

"If you would only wait until an American with much money married you," Penelope said, "then we would make visits at each other's houses every day, and I would give you slices of cake with as much honey as you could eat, and—and *peaches.*"

"But I love Demetrios," Thalia said.

"Why do you love him?"

"He is good, and that is better than riches."

"You will have to sleep outdoors the year round."

"No," Thalia said. "Demetrios has found a little house for us. He will pay the Miller a bushel of wheat a year for it. And in the summer we shall live in Demetrios' new shack. It has two whole stories, my Penelope, and is made out of grass and reed. And I shall make a pergola in front, and plant jasmine and pomegranates. All day long we shall feel the good sun and the wind in our faces, and smell the pine woods, and at night we shall hear the nightingale sing."

"I suppose Demetrios is *almost* as good as an American," Penelope said, doubtfully.

"I am very lucky," Thalia said; "my three elder sisters have married, so now I may, too. I shall bring to my husband nut and olive trees, blankets, and a chest." Thalia stood up. "See this fine red dye for Perseus' tunic? It came from the holly oak in Kyr Mihale's garden." Thalia held up the little red garment. "There, it is all done; carry it home with the mask and the pouch for Nikias. And mind you, Penelope, have a care; you carry a god's raiment."

"Bah, it will be like *living* with a god now," Penelope said in a very grown-up voice. She really wasn't quite sure what a god was.

Thalia laughed.

"You tell him he must bring luck for Demetrios and me with those winged sandals," she said.

Going down the cobblestone street, near the village square, Penelope met Papous just coming out of the coffee shop.

"Oh, Papous," she called, "I am carrying Perseus."

"I will help you," Papous said, laughing.

"No," Penelope said.

Perhaps, after all, one had to be careful with a god.

49

Chapter Six

MEANWHILE Demetrios and Nikias were sitting under the plane tree high in the sheepfold, talking about aeroplanos. Using a small sharp knife, Demetrios was whittling a tiny propeller, humming his shepherd's song as he worked. Nikias lay on his stomach, his elbows on the ground, his face in his hands, watching.

"Isn't the right wing a slight bit smaller?" he asked, anxiously.

"No, my little birdman, it is the slant at which I hold it."

"If I were driving my aeroplano, and I ran into kicking winds, what should I do, Demetrios?"

"Hold the stick steady. That is good advice always." Demetrios pushed over a newspaper. "There, look at that picture; does it not seem just like this little airship?"

"Papous says that in case we have war our country will need many aeroplanos," Nikias said, looking at the picture.

"Yes, but it takes a long time to make a flyer, to say nothing of the ships."

"Demetrios, it is a brave thing, isn't it, to fly when the floor is made of clouds?"

"Some say that when God shakes His head and there is an earthquake it is even worse on earth, but, for me, I intend to remain on the good soil. There is too much hurry in aeroplanos."

"I hope it will be finished when Paolos comes," Nikias said, proudly, looking at the model. "Who knows, perhaps he has never seen one so small."

"Oh, ho! There you are wrong," laughed Demetrios. "Do you not know that America built the first airship?"

"Perseus did," Nikias said.

"It is a long way from winged sandals to a great aeroplano driven by engines. Icarus, now, he was a step closer."

"Icarus! Who was he?"

"A hero of Greece, but I have not time now to tell you the story; it must keep." Demetrios was polishing the tiny tail fin of the plane.

"Oh, if I could only see a real aeroplano!" Nikias said. "But our village is too far from the great cities. Demetrios wouldn't there be time for just a *little* more about Perseus?"

"Well, I cannot tell you much. See, the sun will soon go down, and you must be setting off."

"Tell me what happened after Perseus turned Atlas into stone."

"He came then to the country of the Ethiopians. The queen there had made one of the sea nymphs angry, and she had sent a sea serpent to attack the cities that lay beside the sea. Only in one way would this sea nymph forgive the queen."

51

"How was that?"

"For Andromeda, the princess, to be chained to a rock, and the sea serpent devour her."

Nikias shivered. "And—did it?" he asked.

"You move too fast! Perseus found Andromeda chained to the rock. She was sitting so still that except for her tears, she might have been a marble statue. For a moment Perseus was so surprised he almost forgot to flap his wings—"

"He would have drowned?"

"That he would. Never forget to use your wings when you fly, Nikias."

"But I haven't any."

"No? Well, Perseus remembered just in time, and whispered to the maiden that he would rescue her if she would agree to marry him. She thereupon promised—Perseus was a likely-looking lad—and just then Perseus saw the serpent swimming toward him. He flew high, threw a rock at its back, and—"

"Killed him?"

"No, but the story goes, he made blood come from a great wound, and the serpent thrashed the water. Then, swift as an eagle, Perseus flew onto the serpent's back, and seized it by the neck. *There* was a fight, I tell you! The serpent tried to drive his fangs into Perseus' body, but Perseus, using his wings, flew into the air so the serpent could not reach him. Then he drew his sword and—"

"And the serpent was dead?"

"Yes, my Nikias, as dead as this fly here. And the king

and the queen and all the people were very happy, as who would not be, and there was a great feast when Perseus married the maiden."

"Like the one you will have next week, Demetrios?"

"Not to be compared with it! *I* shall feed on humming-birds' tongues, and——"

But Demetrios never finished the words, for just at that moment they heard a great buzzing sound. It was like a million hornets in a clover field, and it seemed to come straight from out of the sky. Both Demetrios and Nikias jumped to their feet. They looked up, shielding their eyes from the sun. The sound grew louder and louder, and a minute later there came riding out of the white clouds straight above their heads—an aeroplano. There were great silver stripes on the wings, and a blue and white emblem, and the body was gray. The thunder of the motors grew so great that it seemed almost to drown their breathing.

"Virgin Mary, but it is an aeroplano!" cried Demetrios.

"An aeroplano!" Nikias said in a whisper. He was so excited he thought his heart was going to stop beating.

"A beauty, is she not?" cried Demetrios in a great shout. He jumped up and down, waving his arms. "See how she drives through the clouds! Listen to her engines speak!"

"Oh! Oh! She has gone!" Nikias said.

"What luck is ours!" Demetrios said. "The gods are kind. We talk of an aeroplano, and there is one sent to us straight from Heaven."

"An aeroplano, an aeroplano!" Nikias whispered.

54

Chapter Seven

IT WAS the day of the Masquerade, and Demetrios was on his way to the village. He was not alone. Ever since the sun had come up over the rosy mountain peaks, people from the hills and valleys had begun to flock to the village. They came on mules and donkeys that wore gay ribbons about their necks; they came, just like the Greeks of a thousand years before, bundled into little bright red wagons with solid wooden wheels, drawn by patient oxen; and they came on foot. Demetrios could see the many things they carried: food, bedding, music. Sometimes whole lambs were tied on the backs of the donkeys, to be roasted later on spits. In the double baskets, called panniers, that were carried by the donkeys, were fresh greens, chickens, pots of honey, eggs, cheese, rice, garlic, and fresh-baked whole-wheat bread.

Demetrios knew that the people brought blankets so they could spend the night in comfort in the village. Most of them would lie out under the stars and the little sickle moon. Some lucky ones would stay in the houses of relatives and friends. Many of the women with babies and small children were invited to sleep in the church.

How shining-clean everyone looked for the feast day,

Demetrios thought. The women wore new veils, and aprons gaily embroidered in bright colors. The men's *fustanellas* were starched and pleated for the occasion, and their white socks had brave red stitches. The poorer ones wore smocks and some of them had on European clothes. All the fezzes were trimmed with new tassels, and the shoes with red and blue pompons. They made a very fine array. Everyone was gay and happy, eager to hear the news of the village, and to give his own; most eager of all to join in the merrymaking.

Demetrios had driven his flock down to a lower level so that the young boy he had hired might watch more safely in case a fox or a wolf attacked. Demetrios had given him thirty cents for the ten hours he was to watch; he knew it was good wages. With a shepherd dog at each side of the line, the goats and sheep had moved in an orderly way, whenever they heard Demetrios' voice, stopping still and even lying down.

Demetrios himself was brave in his *fustanella,* blue jacket, and white cloak. About his waist in a pouch he carried his pistol, his knife, and the reed. His staff, curved at the end so that he could catch the necks of disobedient sheep, was in his hand.

When he came to the village it was noon. The streets were full of people, laughing, singing, talking. In fact there was so much noise he could not hear the voice of the little waterfall that he liked so well. The houses were decorated with wreaths of early spring flowers, and every window sill had a pot of sweet basil or a blooming plant. The booths in the market place were set out with wares of food and drink, with amber beads and bright kerchiefs. Peddlers were calling their wares: "Ho, buy pitchers! Big pitchers, little pitchers, all the way from Aegina!" The candyman's sing-song voice was droning: "I have *baklava*, sesame, and *pastelli*. Who wants to buy my sweetmeats?" He was doing a brisk trade among the children in sugar almonds wrapped in pink muslin, because these cost less than a penny. "How much?" "How much?" People were asking the question at every booth. In one stall there were needles, thread, dyes made from wild plants and holly berries, and embroidery silk all the way from France. It was here Demetrios found Thalia and Penelope. Thalia was laughingly trying to decide whether to buy red silk or purple.

Demetrios tweaked one of Penelope's curls. She looked very pretty in a white linen skirt and a blue jacket with red embroidery at the armholes and hem. Manitza had been careful to rub a bit of soot behind her ear and on the fold of her skirt, lest bad luck come to her if people praised her pretty face or the fine new dress.

"May the holy Virgin be with you," Demetrios said to Thalia, smiling happily.

"The good hour to you," Thalia said.

"And how is your health?" Demetrios asked Penelope. "With all these pranksters about, you had best watch out the hobgoblins don't catch you."

"I shall owe it to you as a favor," said Penelope, who

liked to use grown-up words, "if you will go with Thalia and me to see the dancing."

"Oh, yes, we will just be in time," Thalia said.

"But where is Nikias?" asked Demetrios, looking around.

"A minute ago I saw Theo asking him to match pennies," Penelope answered. "If Manitza catches him he will go supperless to bed."

"Oh, ho," said Demetrios, "the boy must have his fun now and then. Is it not Lent tomorrow with long faces all about, and no meat or eggs to eat? Come, we'll find those dancers."

In the open square a dance called the *Syrlos* was just beginning. A young man was the leader. In his left hand he held a bright handkerchief, which was held by a girl with her right. And in this way they made a long winding chain. Thalia and Demetrios were near the end. Now they began to sing. To an American, the voices would have sounded very shrill and out of tune, but to Penelope, watching, it was wonderful. Was not Kyr Mihale playing his mandolin for them, the quill picking out the rollicking tune? The chain began to wind around and around, the dancers lifting first one foot, then the other. The dance ended with a great shout, and then everybody crowded about Kyr Mihale, begging for a song. Smiling, he agreed, and soon everyone was singing a mountain air. High above the others Penelope could hear Demetrios' voice. He knew the old mountain songs as well as he did the stories of Greece.

Penelope listened a while and then she wandered off. She felt as if she could hardly wait until tonight when the costume parade would be held. She was going to be a rabbit. Thalia had made her beautiful pointed ears lined with pink, a stubby little bunny tail, and even whiskers. Penelope had been practicing springing and jerking her head for so long that she felt enough like a rabbit to live on lettuce leaves for the rest of the year.

She found Manitza at the home of the Miller. She was sitting under a mulberry tree talking to the Miller's jolly wife. The Miller's house, Penelope knew, was the great one of the village. It had two stories, glazed windowpanes instead of just wooden shutters, a balcony, and a pergola with vines clambering over it. Behind the house, up on the hill, were three windmills.

"Tell me," the Miller's wife was saying, "have Thalia and Demetrios killed the lamb?"

"Aye, and sprinkled its blood on the ground where the new hut is built," Manitza said. "Sit you down, Penelope; your face is hot."

"Those two know well the old customs," the Miller's wife said, smiling at Penelope, and patting her hand.

Manitza's little head went from side to side.

"It is true. Thalia's good mother had taught her well. She knows that there are certain days when one may not cut one's nails; that it is bad luck to let eggs go out of one's house after sunset, and that one must never speak angry words with bread in one's hands."

59

"I suppose that kinsman of yours, young Paolos, will laugh at our old ways," the Miller's wife said. "Do you know yet the day he will come?"

"The good God willing, in a few weeks now," Manitza answered.

"I should be glad to have your luck, welcoming a grandson like that one. America must be a country full of miracles."

"From all accounts it is a wonderful place," said Manitza, "but I like best our own Greece." She sighed and looked down at her little dark withered hands. "God grant we may not have war," she said. "This morning my husband heard a hen crow like a cock, and that means bad luck."

"You are sure its head was not turned to the east?" the Miller's wife asked; "then all would have been well."

Manitza made the little thrusting movement of the chin that means no in Greece.

The Miller's wife sighed, and then she laughed. "Well, let us not talk of such things on a day like this," she said. "Look at that little Penelope. I vow she is like a lamb in spring; she cannot keep from frisking."

"She waits the Masquerade tonight," Manitza said. "She and Nikias have talked of nothing else for a week. I can tell you, they did not need the swallows' chirpings to wake them *this* morning."

"Well, my little Penelope," said the Miller's wife, "I have a pleasant task for you; go to the coffee shop and tell the Miller and Kyr Yannio, your grandfather, that the food is ready. Can you not smell it? There is *moussaka* slice, and your favorite sweetmeat."

"But where is Nikias?" asked Manitza.

"Oh, I'll find him," Penelope said, and she went dancing off down the street.

As it turned out, Penelope was right; she soon came on Nikias. He and some other boys were gathered about the booth of the traveling snake charmer. The man had a cage full of wriggling snakes of all sizes and colors. He even held one wound around his waist. He was selling powders that he said would prevent snake bites ever hurting you. Nikias and Theo were gazing with open mouths at the man, who was a very dirty and sharp-eyed looking person. Penelope, keeping a safe distance from the snakes, tapped Nikias on the arm.

"Come," she said, "the Miller's good wife has sent me; dinner is ready. I go to find Papous at the coffee shop."

Nikias followed Penelope with a lagging step. There were so many exciting things all taking place at the same time that he was afraid of missing one of them.

Inside the coffee shop they found a crowd of men gathered around Papous.

"The Frankos, the outsiders," Papous was saying, "whisper that Greece today is a land without courage; its people lazy, not knowing the way they go. On my father's soul, I hope they are wrong."

The Miller shook his head, meaning that he agreed.

"You are right, Kyr Yannio," he said; "there are

troubled days ahead for Greece. I pray we will prove ourselves worthy of our past."

Nikias stood there listening. It was a very silly feeling, of course, but he thought that the beautiful purple shadow that the sun had been making on the flags outside the door had suddenly turned black. That was stupid. Was he living in a fairy tale where the goblins played pranks? No, it was *today*, and today was the Masquerade. Was not his Perseus costume waiting there at home for him? He felt very happy again; he wanted to dance and laugh. Just wait until they saw him tonight! Wouldn't they clap their hands and cheer when they looked at those sandals with the wings? They would say: "There was a brave man! Nikias, he means to be just like Perseus, too, when he is grown."

Why, everything was all right; of course it was. Nikias put his hand in Papous', as they started down the street toward the Miller's house.

There was a feast not to forget for a long time! The Miller's wife was known as a great hand at cooking. The *moussaka* slices were made of mincemeat and rich butter and eggs, but the cake that Nikias liked best had honey in it mixed with flour and milk. Just to look at the great skin bags of cheese was enough to make Papous' mouth water. And to end the meal, weren't there figs and almonds and rich, strong coffee that Manitza loved?

During the rest hour neither Nikias nor Penelope slept a wink. Even if the nymph should catch them walking in the hot sun, they weren't going to waste any of this big day, not they! And besides, Nikias remembered, hadn't Demetrios promised to tell stories under the mulberry tree at Thalia's house? There would be many people there, of course, because Demetrios was known as the village story-teller or rhapsodist. A rhapsodist, Nikias knew, was one who loves to tell of the glories of his country, of the brave deeds of its heroes and the beauties of the mountains, seas, and valleys. But Nikias thought to himself that Demetrios would be looking at him some of the time he was talking. Were they not great friends? They had watched the sheep in the lonely fold in the mountains for many an hour together. Demetrios had even shown him how you put the tongue against the teeth when you whistled for the sheep. Did they not share that great moment when the aeroplano passed in the white clouds? And did not Demetrios know all about the Perseus costume that he, Nikias, was going to wear tonight?

But when Nikias got to Thalia's house, Demetrios was not telling any tales out of the *Arabian Nights* or the *Iliad;* he was describing a place called the Hanging Monasteries, and telling of the great Mount Olympus, the highest peak in Greece. He was saying a verse about Old Man Olympus and his forty-two peaks, and the sixty springs, and the treasures that lay hidden in his rocks. Everybody listened without a sound, except for the little click-click their fingers made playing with their beads.

When Demetrios had finished, Theo asked him to tell a story about the Turks and the way they had fought the

Greeks, and of course Demetrios did. He was always doing things for people. Nikias wanted to hear more about Perseus. Had he married Andromeda and lived happily ever after? Or were there more monsters for him to fight? Nikias lay on his stomach in the warm sun, propping his face in his hands, listening and thinking. One of these days, instead of wearing winged sandals, perhaps he would be a great birdman flying an aeroplano.

Chapter Eight

IT WAS getting dark. Nikias, standing beside the open door as Manitza tied the belt about his tunic, saw that the houses all over the village were dotted with little lights like so many fireflies. Nikias' feet would not keep still; they wanted to whirl and dance. For were not the winged sandals laced on those feet? The wings were a beautiful silver, the tunic a soft dark brown. The little traveling hat on Nikias' head was just like the one Perseus had worn two thousand years before, and in his hand was the sickle sword that the god Hermes had given Perseus before he set out on his adventures.

He felt exactly like Perseus. Why he *was* Perseus! He felt brave and strong and full of adventuring thoughts. If Penelope had only been Andromeda chained to that rock, he thought, instead of a little pink-eared rabbit playing with its white whiskers, he would have rescued *her* with one stroke of his paper sword. If Vias, the hound, were the giant Atlas, instead of a lazy dog sleeping beside the fireplace, he would have turned *him* into stone with a single whisk of the Gorgon's head. Papous had told him he ought to cut off a hen's head (one they would make into soup tomorrow) and carry it for the Gorgon, but even Nikias could not

65

imagine anyone turning into stone when he looked at the little wizened hen's head. Perhaps Demetrios, with a great laugh, might have pretended *he* was; but that would be all.

"There, you are ready," Manitza said.

She was looking at Nikias standing there, his feet straddled wide apart, his sword brandished, with a funny look on her wrinkled face. It almost seemed as if she had to squeeze up her eyes so two tears wouldn't show.

"Be sure you *act* like Perseus," Papous said. He was sitting smoking his clay pipe just outside the door.

"Nikias' costume is not nearly as pretty as mine," Penelope said, happily twirling her long white whiskers.

"What is your first adventure with the winged sandals to be, Nikias?" Manitza asked.

"I—I shall kill dragons for Demetrios," Nikias said.

"And for Thalia," said Penelope. She gave an excited squeal. "Oh, oh, look! The parade, it's coming!"

"Aye," said Papous. "I can hear the drum and the fiddle."

"Hurry, hurry!" Penelope cried. "We will be late."

Penelope pulled impatiently at Nikias' arm, but Nikias felt that his feet were stuck to the floor. They wouldn't move.

"Hark, child," Manitza said to Penelope, "there is time and to spare. Do you not know that the masked ones will stop first at a dozen houses?"

"And they will give us cakes and sweetmeats?" asked Penelope.

"Yes. And do not forget, my little rabbit, that I have rubbed soot on your leg so that overmuch praise may not harm you."

"Be on your way, my revelers," Papous said, smiling.

And then Penelope had her hand in Nikias', and Nikias gave himself a little shake, and the two were running down the street as fast as their feet would carry them.

The masqueraders were nearly all in line. Kyr Mihale was finding places, giving orders, trying to calm the excited voices. There was Theo in his huntsman's dress, looking very fierce and frowning. There was Thalia with a deer's mask on her head, and Demetrios wearing his own sheep's mask, with a comic tail tied to his back, and his nose painted black. The drum began a great rat-a-tat; the pipes began to scream. Kyr Mihale's mandolin started a rollicking tune, and away the procession started.

What fun it was! Everyone laughed and sang and talked. It was open house night; there was not a door closed. Soon it would be dull Lent; tonight they would make merry. In the square the procession broke up into little bands and danced and danced. Pranks were played; there were jokes aplenty. Demetrios dropped a small green snake down Theo's back, and one of the boys seized a bow and arrow and made believe he was shooting it. Nobody worried about anything. The Miller played leap frog over the fat body of Thalia's father, and even the Pappas roared with laughter at the sight. Someone started a song, and Demetrios got out his reed and played. Then they all marched up to the Mil-

67

ler's house where there were sweetmeats enough even for Theo, and the Miller poured earthen cups of wine for the men. Nikias and Penelope munched their goodies, and sang and laughed, and were very happy.

And so the merry evening wore on, till the great moment came. In the center of the market square stood the three judges, the Pappas, Kyr Mihale, and the Miller, ready to decide which was the best costume. And the prize was a beautiful book with gold lettering on the cover. It was called the *Iliad,* and was about the heroes of old Greece. Hadn't the Miller sent all the way to Athens for it at the suggestion of Kyr Mihale? There was a rolling of the drum, and the marchers were herded in a line that began to move slowly in front of the judges. Round and round in a circle they went now, passing a half-dozen times in front of the three men. The Miller and the Pappas put their heads together and frowned, as if they were very perplexed at their task, but Kyr Mihale stood there with his arms crossed, as if he had made up his mind and didn't care even to talk about it.

Then suddenly the Pappas held up his hand, and the music stopped, and everyone was quite still.

"Never since the Gordian knot was cut," said the Pappas, "has there been so hard a task set three judges." Everyone was looking at the Pappas. He wore his long black robe and his headdress that was like a stovepipe. "Never have there been so many and so excellent costumes on Masquerade Day. Our task has been hard. But at last we have made up our minds. There is one costume that brings back the

70

great past of our land; it is that of Perseus, the winged warrior. I have, therefore, the pleasure of declaring that Nikias Yannio is the winner of the prize."

Nikias thought he was going to choke; his breath wouldn't come. His hands were very cold; his feet didn't feel as if they wore wings; they were just like the lumps of ice on the little pond at wintertime. Then Nikias felt Demetrios nudging him, saying, "Where are your winged sandals, my Nikias?" And there he was stumbling across the cobblestones toward the judges.

"Both for the great Perseus who showed the courage that saved his country from its enemies, and for the little Perseus," the Pappas said, smiling. And there was the beautiful book lying in Nikias' hands.

Then it happened. Theo dug his elbows into the side of the boy standing next him.

"Ho, but that is a joke," he said in a loud voice, "Nikias winning a prize for bravery. That one, he runs if a mouse comes!"

And Theo gave a great laugh. A minute later the boy next to him was laughing, too, and then the laugh seemed to run right down the line of children as if it had been so much electricity. They only laughed because they wanted a reason to laugh, but then one of the men standing behind Theo (who was sure his costume of a mountain goat should have won) gave a loud laughing sound, too, and presently the whole crowd were shouting, leaning their hands on their knees, pointing, digging one another's ribs. That is, all of them were except Demetrios, Thalia, Penelope, and the judges.

But Nikias didn't stop to notice that. It seemed to him that the laughing was just like a great wind that was taking away his breath. He could feel his wings tumbling down beside his sandals; he could see his sword crumpling at his side. He, Nikias, pretending to be Perseus, the brave! That was funny. That was a great joke. *Everybody* thought so— everybody. He was shamed before that big crowd; he was nothing but a laughingstock. Demetrios would never care to be his friend again. The boys at school would point their finger at him. Kyr Mihale would never again let him read out loud the stories of the heroes of Greece.

Nikias took the book, threw it on the ground, and, his hands in his face, went running, stumbling down the street toward home.

Chapter Nine

I T WAS dark and still inside the house. It was very late. Papous and Penelope had gone to bed and to sleep an hour before. Nikias, too, was lying in his bed. But he wasn't sleeping. Manitza had heard his soft sobs from the other side of the room. She had got up, lighted the oil wick in the tumbler, and now was kneeling beside Nikias' blanket.

"Nikias, Nikias," she said, "you must not cry."

But Nikias did not speak; he just sobbed on.

"You weep because those silly ones laughed when you received the prize? Is that it? But, hark you, all they looked for was a reason to laugh and make merry; is it not carnival day?"

"Theo, he—" began Nikias, and then his tears stopped him.

"Theo would have liked that prize himself, I will warrant. Besides, he is a little one who does not stop to think what he will say; his fists, they think for him."

"They—they laughed at me," Nikias said in a whisper.

"No, no; *with* you they laughed, my Nikias. They were glad for you. Penelope, she told me what the Pappas said."

74

"They were right to laugh, Manitza; I am not such a one as Perseus."

"Do you think to be brave means one must have a fighter's muscles?"

"Perseus fought," Nikias said.

"Hark, you, many of the brave deeds of the world have been fought in the heart, without a blow or the sound of gunpowder."

"Manitza, I wanted to fly high in the clouds—"

"Some people must fight *themselves* before they are brave. It is as if there were giants inside them. You are one of these, my Nikias."

"Manitza, will you make a fire and burn—burn my wings and the little hat—so I shall never see them again? Will you, Manitza?" Nikias whispered.

Manitza looked at Nikias.

"*I* believe in you, my Nikias," she said. "Remember that."

"You *do,* Manitza?"

"Yes, my son. Now, dry your tears. Do you wish Paolos to find his cousin one who goes to his dreams with tears?"

"N-no, Manitza."

"Come, then, I will sing you your shepherd's song while you close your eyes. Tomorrow you will go to Kyr Mihale, to the Pappas and the Miller, and tell them you were wrong to let fall the book, and beg for it again."

Nikias gave a little sigh. Manitza's voice was just like the soft twittering of the swallows when it was night. Nikias closed his eyes, and she sang, and presently he slept.

The next day when the boys and girls sat in a circle about Kyr Mihale, he said, "Today you will not study your multiplication table. Today I shall tell you a story." And he began:

"More than a thousand years ago the Lord Jesus was crucified. A few men knew beforehand that so great a wrong would be, and some *things* knew. The trees of the forest knew. They live all day close to God's breath, the wind; and to the sky, His footstool; and to the stars, His candles. So that one day they heard that a cross, upon which the Saviour would hang, was to be carved from one of their hearts. And they made a vow: never would they allow any woodcutter to touch their wood to make this cross. If he did so they would turn away from the blow, or blunt the edge of the ax. But one tree did not make this vow; it was the ilex, or winter oak, as we call it in these parts. It agreed to let the cross be carved from its heart. And so it was. But today the woodcutters in our mountains will not soil their ax with the wood of the ilex, nor will they let it burn upon their hearths."

Kyr Mihale stopped and looked over toward the corner of the room where Nikias and Theo sat. He spoke unhurriedly, as he did everything.

"There are many kinds of courage," he said, "but that of the trees and the woodcutters is the hardest to possess, because no drum plays for it, and no flags fly. Now we will turn to the spelling lesson. Theo, you may spell the word 'Greece.' "

76

Chapter Ten

KYR MIHALE had just finished his meal of rice and spinach, washed down with a glass of wine, and was thinking happily of the new book about the government that had come that day from his brother in Athens, when there came a knock at the door. Opening it, Kyr Mihale saw Papous and Manitza standing there. All Greeks like visitors and, besides, Kyr Mihale was fond of old Manitza, while he liked nothing better than to talk with Papous about the affairs of the world. He smiled and invited them to enter. He did not shake hands because that is seldom done in Greece.

"May all your dead become saints," he said.

"And the good hour be with you," answered Papous.

"There was a chill in the air, so I have lighted a fire," said Kyr Mihale. "Draw close and I will consider it a pleasure if you will accept an almond cake and a draught of wine."

He went to the back of the room, and came back with the food.

"The spring begins to smile," Manitza said politely. "Sooner than we know, Easter will be here and then May Day with its wreaths and songs."

"Your almond cakes are good enough for a feast day, Kyr Mihale," Papous said.

"Only today I bought from the Miller my first bag of meal," Kyr Mihale said. "I pray you, Kyra Yannio, open the bag, since it will bring me good luck to have one who has christened a child do this thing."

"It makes my heart glad to know a man who still keeps the old customs," Manitza said. "You are a son to bring honor to Greece."

"I hope so," said Kyr Mihale, very pleased.

"The Miller showed me his granary today," said Papous. "The sight made me impatient for St. George Day to come so that I may walk in the fields with the Pappas and see how fares the wheat."

"Now if the good God will but untie the goatskin and pour out some rain, we shall have crops to warm the heart," Kyr Mihale said.

Manitza drew out a jacket of dark blue that she was making for Penelope, and began to sew. Kyr Mihale rattled the glass beads he wore around his neck.

"If war comes," said Papous, "every grain of wheat will be worth so much gold."

Manitza walked over to where the little lamp burned under the eikon, crossed herself, and made a silent prayer.

"May the good Virgin grant we have no war," she said.

"Tomorrow will be the marriage of Demetrios and Thalia," said Kyr Mihale. "They have chosen the last day before Lent."

78

"Their marriage can but bring happiness to both," said Papous.

And then no one said anything for a minute. Kyr Mihale knew that his visitors had come to tell him something, and would do it when they saw fit, because it is the way in Greece to take your time. Presently Manitza spoke.

"Do me a favor and may you enjoy your life, Kyr Mihale," she said.

"I shall owe it to you as a kindness if you will lend your ear," Papous said.

"Yes?" said Kyr Mihale, wondering what was coming.

"The matter has to do with our grandson, Nikias," Manitza said slowly.

Papous frowned into the little fire of holly logs.

"The matter lies close to our hearts," he said.

"I pray you go on," said Kyr Mihale. What had his favorite pupil done now? No one spoke then, and Kyr Mihale thought: Has it something to do with what happened yesterday at the Masquerade? "The trouble between Nikias and Theo is mended," he said. "Also Nikias has said he is sorry about the book; I have cleaned off the dirt from the cover and given it once more to the boy."

"The trouble is not mended," said Manitza. Kyr Mihale saw that her sewing had fallen into her lap.

"Nikias," said Papous, "has a hunger for learning—"

"That we cannot feed," finished Manitza.

"You mean his wish to fly?" asked Kyr Mihale.

Papous shook his head to mean yes.

79

"In the old days," he said, "our young men were taught skill in running and jumping and throwing the javelin. I am a poor man with little learning myself; the tales of old Greece lie locked in my memory as my father taught them to me, but of such matters as flying, I know nothing."

"There must be many years of study to make a man a pilot," said Kyr Mihale. "My brother, the one who lives in Athens, tells me they must attend the gymnasium first, and then go to a great college where they learn mathematics and machinery and about the stars."

"Of stars I know nothing," said Papous, "save to tell the time just as my fathers did."

"How much would it take for this learning?" Manitza asked.

"Much gold, I fear," answered Kyr Mihale, sadly.

"We have only the means to let him go to the lower school for four years," Manitza said in a low voice; "there is nothing saved in the wooden chest for lessons at the gymnasium. There is the little Penelope's dowry to think of, too."

"We have few goods," said Papous, looking down, "but we must leave Nikias such things that will feed his heart."

" 'Tis as if a goblin had put a spell on the boy," said Manitza; "he is both brave and afraid."

"No goblin has our Nikias," said Kyr Mihale. "It is the good God that has set him a battle to wage in his own heart."

"One day of late," said Manitza, "he and Demetrios saw

an aeroplano high in the sky. Now the little one talks of it in his sleep."

Papous was standing up. His old shoulders looked bent and tired.

"Come," he said to his wife, "it is time we went; we must not weary the good Kyr Mihale with our troubles."

Manitza obediently folded up the little jacket and put it in her *tagari*.

"Good night to you, Kyr Mihale," she said.

Chapter Eleven

"So lovely is your flaxen hair,
So long and gold and gleaming,
That only angels, they may dare
To comb its yellow streaming."

PENELOPE was brushing out Thalia's long hair,
singing this song as she worked. It was Thalia's
wedding day. Everything was ready. Thalia's
mother was bustling about the house, setting things in
place, making ready the feast for the guests. The little cot-

tage was full of fragrant smells. Even the garden seemed to know there was a wedding. The lilies, crocuses, and hyacinths were pushing up between their green leaves, just as if they were throwing off so much winter clothing. There were neat little borders of parsley and rue, and Thalia's favorite mulberry tree, where she sat and spun and wove on her loom, was full of pretty dappled shadow. Probably even the birds had heard of the wedding, because the garden was full of their peepings and twitterings. The garden, too, was full of guests. They were Thalia's relatives and friends, and they had come from far and near for the wedding. Now they were wandering about, hopefully sniffing at the rich, spicy smells that came pouring out through the open door.

One of Thalia's bridesmaids was setting flowers in earthenware jars, straightening the eikons on the wall, putting the furniture and bedding in place. The other, the older one, was smoothing out the bride's fresh white dress, with its jacket of embroidered velvet, its headdress of muslin with a band of shining coins.

"Have you set out the 'necessary spoonfuls'?" Thalia asked her mother.

Penelope stopped brushing. "What are 'necessary spoonfuls'?" she said.

"Silly little one," said the younger of the bridesmaids; "have you not heard about the weasel?"

"No," said Penelope.

"The legend goes that she was once a bride herself, and

then was turned into a weasel. Ever since she has been envious of brides."

"But how silly of her," said Penelope, staring.

"She is said to take it out by spoiling wedding gifts and food," explained Thalia. "So we set a bowl of sweetmeats and honey outside the door, and sing a song, begging her to eat and spare the wedding things."

"Oh, ho, what fun!" cried Penelope, clapping her hands, "I wish *I* were a bride and had a jealous weasel."

They all laughed, and Thalia gave Penelope a loving hug.

"Come, children, stop your chatter," called Thalia's mother. "We must eat now. See, the table is already set under the mulberry tree. I am putting the mutton on the platter this very minute."

"Oh, make haste, Thalia," said the older bridesmaid, "you must be starting for church very soon; the Pappas and the best man will be calling for you."

"But I must sing the little song as I slip Thalia's dress over her head," said the younger bridesmaid. And she started to sing these words:

> "Today the flowers are open,
>   The sky is fair above,
> Today it is the wedding
>   'Tween the eagle and the dove."

Soon everyone was seated around the long table. That is, everybody except the bridegroom and the best man.

84

Thalia was just like a princess, Penelope thought. The guests had all brought her gifts. There were lambs and goats, tied with gay ribbons; food and embroidered aprons and kerchiefs. The table was loaded with good things. There were great cheeses in goatskins; roasted mutton; curds of thick sour milk; olives, onions, potatoes, okra; and for dessert, delicious sweetmeats and a round cake made with mincemeat, eggs, and butter.

Everyone laughed and was gay and told jokes. Nikias sat next to Manitza, but Penelope was almost too important to be spoken to. Had she not a seat right next to Thalia, the bride? Was she not herself one of the bridesmaids? And had she not (when Manitza was not looking) washed off the piece of soot behind her ear lest she did not look pretty enough for a bridesmaid?

" 'Tis the only good thing the Turks ever did for Greece, that they left us this *pilaf*," said Papous, helping himself from the bowl of tomatoes, rice, and butter.

"Luck goes with the bride," said Manitza; "when the swallows first flew, she saw the face of Demetrios in the mirror she held over her shoulder."

"It was shining right there in the pool, so all will go well with our Thalia," agreed the eldest sister.

"And our family is truly blessed," said Thalia's mother, "since our three sons have refused to marry until their sisters did."

"Also our little Thalia waited until her older sisters had all married," said Thalia's father, lovingly tweaking her ear.

"What dowry does she bring Demetrios?" asked an aunt. She had rather a long nose that she was a little too fond of poking into other people's business.

"Four nut trees, two olive trees, five blankets, two copper pots, three petticoats, six homespun sheets." It was Thalia's mother speaking proudly. "Have I not woven linen and rugs for her since she was a baby?"

"It is well," said the nosey aunt. She looked a little disappointed that she couldn't find any fault.

"Demetrios is a true son of Greece," said Papous. "He will bring her nothing but happiness."

"And besides she will never know a single dull moment," said the younger bridesmaid, "with a husband who knows by heart all those tales."

Thalia was so excited she could hardly eat, and Penelope, who wanted to be like Thalia in every way, had a hard time now, so good the honey slices tasted, so hungry she was.

"I have told Thalia," said her mother, anxiously, to Manitza, "to remember always to put pounded onions on a wound in case she or Demetrios should hurt themselves away up there in the mountains."

"That is wise," answered Manitza. "But it will be better still if she always carries a potato on her person."

"Oh, ho, you women worry too much," said Thalia's father. "The plant called 'giver-of-good-sheep' will protect them against all ills, from lack of sleep to a stomach ache."

Nikias sat there, eating his cake, saying little. He did not feel quite as merry as the others. Would Demetrios tell him

86

any more stories now? There was a new tale that he had half promised to tell one of these days; would he forget it?

They were all through eating at last. Everyone was talking at the same time; it sounded just like so many magpies in a mulberry tree. Thalia's mother and sisters were setting the food inside. The bridesmaids were smoothing Thalia's hair, setting on the headdress. Penelope was dancing around in everyone's way. Then down the street they heard the sound of footsteps coming, and there were the Pappas and the best man striding up the path. These two would lead the procession to the church.

Everyone fell in line, and soon they were going into the little church that smelled of flowers. There Demetrios and his parents and friends were waiting, and the service began.

After a while it was over, and again the procession formed, but this time with the bride and groom in the lead; this time to go to the home of Demetrios' parents. It was a beautiful day. The new wedding clothes looked bright against the sparkling blue sky.

At Demetrios' house there were dances and games and then everyone sat down to a second feast with a table just as full of good things. That is everyone sat down except Thalia. She stood in a corner, not even looking up, until dinner was nearly half over. Then the best man went to her, threw back her veil, and led her over to the seat next to Demetrios.

Under the noise of laughing voices and the bleat of the

fiddle, Demetrios whispered to Thalia the words of this old song:

"You are like a red, red rose
Blooming on a tree,
Even if you have a thorn,
'Twill never prick me."

After the meal was over there was still more merrymaking. Even the old white-haired Pappas, who you might think would have fainted in those heavy black clothes, tied up the long beard that reached to his waist, and joined in the fun.

But after a while the shadows began to come. Demetrios and Thalia had to start for their new home. Thalia had just gone to light a wick from the lamp under the eikon so that there would be good luck for her new home, when she felt Penelope tugging at her sleeve.

"Here is my present, Thalia," she said. "See, I saved it to the last." She held up two little bunches of bells with bright-red embroidered leaves. "They are to tie about the ears of your new black mule," she said. "I have made the embroidery all by myself."

"I am the happiest girl in Greece," Thalia said, and she kissed Penelope. "It is because I have so many friends, and am marrying the best man in all the world."

"The weasel did not touch anything," Penelope said. "I looked to see."

"No, she didn't," Thalia said. "I looked, too."

"Thalia," said Penelope, "I am your bridesmaid, and you can tell me *all* your secrets; is there *nothing* you wanted that you didn't get?"

"You are a funny little one," said Thalia. "Could anyone *wish* for more fine gifts?" And then she stopped and gave a little quick sigh. "Well, perhaps there is *one* thing."

"What is it?" Penelope asked.

"I would have liked a rocking chair for the new home—just like those they have in America."

"Oh," said Penelope. Then she thought a second and said, "When I am a grown woman and am married to an American man, with a weasel of my own, I will buy you one. With *red* cushions, Thalia."

It was just at this minute that Nikias, out in the garden, was talking to Demetrios.

"Demetrios," he said, "may your years be full of good."

"And yours, little one," said Demetrios, putting his arms around him.

"Demetrios, could I ask you one favor?"

"Ask on, my friend," said Demetrios, smiling.

"Please do not forget me," said Nikias.

Demetrios laughed a loud laugh, and clapped Nikias on the shoulder.

"On my father's soul," he said, "I would sooner cut off my right ear."

"And—I can come to hear the stories—as before?"

"Have I a listener in all the hills like my Nikias?" asked Demetrios. "Do not talk foolishness."

"I thank you," Nikias said. Then he waited a minute and said, "See, I have a small gift for you."

Demetrios looked at the piece of paper Nikias handed him. It was a drawing that Nikias had made, and it showed two men sitting in an aeroplano, smiling very hard.

"They are you and Perseus driving that aeroplano we saw," said Nikias.

Chapter Twelve

NEARLY a month passed, and it was the Feast of Lazarus, the day that belonged to the children. Easter Day was just a week off.

Nikias and Theo sat just outside the door, carefully tying beautiful spring flowers to a long bamboo shoot. The shoot had soft ends so that it could be bent into a circle. Fastened across it were two bars forming the shape of a Greek cross. The shoot was then tied to a pole. This was called the Lazarus and boys in pairs always trimmed and carried it.

"Ho, but I am glad Lent has passed," said Theo, busily knotting a piece of string around a blue lupine. "No cakes or meat; church songs to learn all day long from the Pappas'; old school gardens to weed."

Nikias bent the bamboo circle a little.

"But we went to see Demetrios five times," he said. "We saw his dog smell out that fox a quarter-mile away, don't you remember? Thalia made us *trahana* one night, and Demetrios let us see those three new baby lambs with the wet black noses."

"Yes, and every five minutes," grumbled Theo, "you were clamoring for one of your old stories. Bah, there is already too much talk in this place for my liking; whispers about the war; whispers about that Paolos of yours who never comes."

"But Paolos may be here *any day*," Nikias said, his cheeks very red.

Penelope looked up from the dress she was making for her stocking doll.

"I for one am glad that Lazarus rose from the dead," she said, "because I like parades. Oh, Nikias, I hope you get hundreds of eggs."

"Ho, I shall get more than he will," Theo boasted. "I am so strong that I expect I shall have to carry the Lazarus pole most of the way myself; all that Nikias is good for is to get high marks from Kyr Mihale at school." Theo sniffed loudly. "And dress up as the brave warrior, Perseus," he said.

Manitza was sitting weaving at her loom. She did not seem to be listening, but she had heard everything the children said.

"Easter is the time when we put new thoughts in our hearts as we set fine new clothes on our backs," she said. "Do not forget that, Theo."

Theo looked sulky, and Nikias hung his head, not saying anything. Then Penelope jumped up and threw her arms around her brother, giving him a big hug.

"Those blue flowers you found for me near the eagle's nest," she said, "will be the beautiful-est in all the parade." She laughed and gave a little skip. "Oh, what a nice man Lazarus is!" she said. "Why is he called the saint of children, Manitza?"

"Perhaps because children's hearts rise out of sorrow just the way Lazarus' body rose from the grave," Manitza said. She smiled. "Look, Theo, what fine new shoes your father made for us all. They are hanging there from the rafters."

"Oh, but wait till you see my new Easter dress with the red and blue embroidery," Penelope said.

"Vain little one," said Manitza laughing. "Has not everyone in the village new clothes from top to toes for Easter?" Manitza got up, and folded the piece of cloth she

93

was weaving. "Look, children, have you not finished that wreath as yet? You must be starting."

Nikias and Theo did not look at one another as they lifted the tall pole between them. Their hands were gripping it very carefully so that it would stand up straight and every flower show on the wreath. As they trudged down the street, Nikias thought of what Manitza had said about children and Lazarus. If a boy's heart forgot to be sad, should it not forget, too, to be angry? He looked at Theo, who was frowning.

"Theo," he said, "the Miller promised me six eggs at his house; I will divide them with you."

"*I* shall be carrying the Lazarus pole when we come to the Miller's," Theo said. "So I shall get *all* the eggs. Why, you cannot even sing the Lazarus song; you have not a fine voice as I have."

"But Nikias is a good singer," Penelope said. "Did not Kyr Mihale promise him an *A* if he would not sing?"

"Ho, did I not tell you," Theo said, "that he sings like a frog in a pond? Anyway, I have more friends than he in the village. Everyone knows what a great wrestler I am."

"Look, look, the procession is forming," Penelope shouted. "Oh, oh, and there is Thalia."

Thalia came up smiling.

"I have good news for you, Nikias," she said. "Demetrios has sent word that he is coming."

"To tell the Lazarus stories with the other shepherds!"

94

Nikias cried. He had forgotten all about everything but his own happiness.

"He will be at the Miller's with the others when the parade is over," Thalia promised. "Think you the Miller would have the Lazarus stories without the best storyteller in the mountains?"

When the parade was over and Nikias began to climb the slope to the Miller's house, he saw that there was already a big crowd of people there, both children and grownups. He felt so happy that he could hardly keep from skipping. Even the day seemed different; since he had heard about Demetrios' coming the flowers smelled sweeter, and the silver-gray olive leaves brighter. The donkeys were shaking their little belled necks, making a tiny merry jingle, and the dogs were barking and gamboling about.

Sitting with his head propped against an almond tree, was Demetrios with Thalia beside him, and near-by four other young shepherds. Piled near them were gifts from the villagers, olive oil, bread and wine, for the villagers knew that shepherds live mostly on wild greens, the fruit of the wild cactus and lupines. Nikias wriggled in among the crowd until he found a spot close to Demetrios. Not far away he saw Penelope, Manitza, and Papous, sitting listening, too. Demetrios was singing a song. He was begging Lazarus to tell what wonders he had seen when he was in the grave those three days. When he stopped a minute, the other shepherds began; they told of the strange sights Lazarus

95

had seen, the sad things and the good things. Then the four shepherds and Demetrios began to sing together.

Nikias was sitting there, his eyes popping out with the things he heard, when he happened to look around. He saw that the crowd was moving, as if it was making way for someone. Then Nikias saw that it was a stranger, and the stranger was coming toward Papous and Manitza. He was a tall young man, wearing the clothes of a European, and he walked as if he hadn't a care in the world. Nikias' heart began to jump. It was—it *must be* Paolos! Nikias couldn't move, he felt so excited. Then he heard a little cry coming from Papous and Manitza, and the two were stretching out their arms toward the stranger.

"Praise be to the holy Virgin!" said Manitza. "It is the son of our son."

"Paolos, is it you?" asked Papous, his voice trembling, and then Nikias saw Manitza throw her arms around the young man's neck; he heard the stranger say in Greek:

"I have a sort of feeling you *must* be my grandmother and grandfather."

Penelope had jumped up, too, and now she was hugging Paolos, and telling him that she was Penelope, his cousin, and the young man was smiling at her and stroking her head. But Nikias felt so shy he still could not move a muscle.

"Come, Nikias." It was Manitza calling him. "Here is your cousin Paolos come at last."

And Nikias was standing in front of Paolos. Only he

96

wasn't looking at him; his eyes were on the ground, his bare toe digging a little hole in the dirt.

"Well, aren't you going to shake hands with me?" asked Paolos.

And Nikias looked up, but he didn't know what to do with the hand Paolos held out to him.

"It is well that you have come," Nikias said in a hoarse voice, and then he looked down at the ground again.

"And what may your name be?" Paolos said, smiling.

"A goblin has stolen his tongue," said Manitza, laughing, and then Demetrios, Thalia, the Miller, Kyr Mihale and all the others were crowding about Paolos, and Manitza and Papous were proudly introducing him.

It was almost a full hour before they could get him home. Penelope was skipping along, already hanging on his arm as if she had known him all her life, and Papous was talking happily, pointing out the sights, telling about the people they passed; while in between Manitza was asking questions about Paolos' father and his mother and that big city called New York. Then they were home. They were sitting him down on a straw chair in front of the door. Manitza was bustling about inside preparing food for supper. Papous was lighting his pipe close beside Paolos. Penelope was leaning against him. Only Nikias stood a little way away, clutching his eggs, too shy to say anything. Paolos looked over at him.

"I'm curious to know what you are doing with all those eggs," he said. "You must be in business with a hen."

Nikias slowly walked toward him, and showed him the

97

eggs. He thought that if Paolos laughed at him, he would just turn and run away. But Paolos did not laugh.

"They are for Easter," Nikias said. "Manitza will color them red."

"I declare!" Paolos said. "I used to do that back in New York when I was a small boy." His voice was warm and friendly, and easy, too; just the way Demetrios talked. "Only we used to paint pictures on ours, and at breakfast on Easter we would see who could eat the most eggs."

"Oh," said Nikias, and then he drew a deep breath and asked, "How—how did you know where to find us?"

"That was easy," Paolos said. "In America whenever we see a crowd, we always find out what it's all about. I saw that mob on the slope, so there I went. What made me curious was the queer clicking sound I heard."

"Oh, that was the beads," Nikias said. "It is the way we do in Greece when we listen or talk."

"Then you must do a lot of listening and talking." Paolos said it in such a funny way with one eyebrow higher than the other, and one side of his mouth pulled down and the other up, that Penelope started to laugh, and presently Nikias was laughing, too. It wasn't more than a minute before he had run into the house and brought back his precious aeroplano, and was showing it to Paolos. Paolos didn't just look at it, say it was very nice, and then put it down, the way most of the grownups did. His eyes got very bright, and he began to touch the tiny wings, the propeller, and the tail fins with gentle fingers.

"This is a model of a bomber, not a passenger plane," he said.

"Papous says you know all about them," Nikias said.

"Well, a little," Paolos said. He laughed and shook back his light hair with a tanned hand. "You see, I've trained to be a pilot. I have a license, and have already flown twenty thousand miles."

"Oh!" said Nikias. "Oh!"

For a minute he couldn't say any more. *Twenty thousand miles!* There was a sort of ringing in his ears. He tried to speak, but he could only swallow. It was as if words were all jammed up in his throat.

"You have taken our Nikias' heart by storm," Papous said, smiling.

"So you are a birdman, too?" asked Paolos.

"I—I—" began Nikias, and then he stopped, and Papous said:

"It is the wish of his life that he fly an aeroplano through the clouds."

Paolos got up. He was such a tall young man that his head almost reached the white flowers of the almond tree. They looked just as if they were his wings, and were tied on to his shoulders, Nikias thought. And then he saw Paolos opening a beautiful shiny black bag, and taking out some packages.

"Then I guessed right for once in my life," he said. "Look, Nikias—this is a model of a passenger plane. I saw it in a store window in New York. Had a notion you might

99

like it. Pretty paint job, isn't it? And here is a doll for you, Penelope; a bit overdressed, *I* thought, but the saleslady said she is wearing the very latest."

There was a squeal from Penelope, but Nikias didn't even hear her. He was holding in his trembling hands the most beautiful little plane he had ever dreamed of. It was made of balsa wood, which is the lightest wood there is, and was painted silver and blue. It had wings as delicate as a butterfly's. There was even a little carved figure in the pilot's seat in front of a shining dashboard. Nikias had just that feeling you have on Christmas morning when you've looked under the tree, and feel you can hardly hold all the happiness inside you.

"I thank you, Cousin Paolos," he said. "I have now two aeroplanos, Demetrios' and yours."

Chapter Thirteen

THE happy week passed. It seemed to Nikias that he was living in one of Demetrios' fairy tales; as if he were walking on rosy air, and eating nothing but sweetmeats and cookies. He was Perseus, and Cousin Paolos had brought him a new pair of winged sandals. The winged sandals were carrying him everywhere, for Paolos told them stories of America, of how the children there lived and played and went to school; of how the big planes, carrying twenty passengers, might be seen a dozen times a day flying over the great white towers of New York.

Paolos went on long walks with Nikias and Penelope; they showed him everything. The third day they even took him up the mountainside to visit Demetrios and Thalia. And Nikias could see from the very first minute that Paolos liked Demetrios, for he asked him all sorts of questions about the sheep and how he lived; he didn't seem to wish to leave him at all. Coming down the mountain, Paolos wanted to know if Demetrios and Thalia ever got lonely, and Nikias said of course not.

Paolos was always asking questions. Nikias and Penelope thought it was great fun answering them; they felt as if they were Kyr Mihale and Paolos just a boy at school.

Paolos asked, "Why is that olive branch hanging on the Miller's door?"

"Because there is a new baby boy there," Penelope said importantly. "If it was a girl, there would be tufts of wool."

"What is the Pappas doing?" he wanted to know.

(It was Good Friday and they were in church.)

"He is putting the eikon from the altar in that casket with all the flowers," Nikias whispered. "Now all the children will go out and sing while it is carried through the streets."

"People will cry, too," Penelope said, "because they are sorry that Christ died."

"But where is Manitza going in such a hurry?" Paolos asked.

"To set a candle in the window," Nikias told him, "so that there will be good luck in our house."

"Why did you crack your red eggs against Penelope's this morning?"

"Oh, because the one whose egg doesn't crack takes both eggs," Nikias explained.

They were going down the street now as they talked. It was Easter day.

Everyone was happy. The church was full of flowers and there was joyful singing. The service was called the love feast. The Pappas read the beautiful words. Do not be angry with anyone, the words said; be generous; forget old grudges. Everyone kissed when they met, and when the

service was over, they carried home lighted candles to light the old lamps kept burning under the eikons.

As they went up the path to the house, Paolos said, "I don't know when I have seen so much happiness."

"Heaven knows, we will need it," Papous said. "I fear the war clouds gather over Greece."

"Now, hark you," said Manitza, "do not talk of such things. Christ has risen! Today spring comes in at the door."

"Manitza is right," said Penelope, who always wanted everything to be cheerful. "You will see, Cousin Paolos; for three days there will be nothing but dancing, songs, and good things to eat."

"Aye," said Manitza. "Paolos, now you will taste our sesame cakes that we eat only at Easter."

"And see the loaves," said Nikias, "that Manitza has baked for the Pappas, with the Greek cross on them, and the sacred seal as well."

"Oh, and the marzipan," cried Penelope, "the almonds, and walnuts and figs with rich cream."

"It sounds just like a sundae," said Paolos, laughing.

"A Sunday?" asked Nikias, perplexed. "But that is the first day in the week."

"Oh, but that isn't all," explained Paolos, laughing. "In America it is something you eat, made of ice cream, and whipped cream and syrup and things."

"I would like well to taste that sundae," said Penelope, with a sigh. "Someday I shall go to America on a big boat, and eat sundaes every day, and rock in a rocking chair, and wear velvet mantillas, and never do any work just like the Americans."

Everyone laughed.

"You've got that all wrong," said Paolos. "Americans work very hard indeed. Why, it seems to me I see more people here sitting in the sun doing nothing except talk than I ever saw in America. Is your exercise talking?"

"You do not understand," said Papous. "Here we have such stony ground that we cannot have great farms like yours in America, so there is not so much to do."

"Then, too," said Manitza, "the Greek people like to take time to listen to the great stories of their past, and to think and wonder about things."

"One does not have to move about like a cricket to be happy," said Papous. "Nor need you have all the money the Americans have to be content."

"*I* like to move like a cricket," said Nikias. "Paolos, cannot we go up the mountain tomorrow and see Demetrios? There is no school and besides I have done all my errands."

"Yes, you have been good children," Manitza said; "you have brought in enough fagots and holly branches for fires for many days to come."

"Paolos," said Nikias, "you have not yet listened to one of his stories."

"It is a fact," Papous put in, "that you will not know our Greece until you hear some of her old tales."

"Oh, please, may I go, too?" begged Penelope.

"Yes, the both of you children may," said Manitza, "if you will start early enough so that it is not dark when you return. I will send Thalia some of my sour-cream cakes."

"I shall waken tomorrow before even the swallows," promised Paolos.

He smiled to himself. He was thinking of a secret he had.

Chapter Fourteen

NEXT morning the three started off up the mountain trail, carrying bread, fruit, and the sourcream cakes. Penelope chattered like a magpie.

"You see that olive tree?" she asked. "It belongs to the Miller." Then after they had climbed for another half-mile, "You see those nut trees? They are the Miller's."

"But how can he keep track of them when they are so far apart?" asked Paolos, surprised.

"Papous says," explained Nikias, "that it is because if someone sees a wild olive tree and grows a *real* olive tree on it, then it becomes his own. It doesn't matter where it is."

A little red wagon passed, drawn by a black mule with pannier baskets on its back. In one was a baby lamb and in the other, vegetables and fruits. Its bells made a merry tinkling sound.

"Look, there are the vineyards," said Penelope. "What fun we will have when we gather the grapes!"

"Our American raisins come from Greece," said Paolos.

"How I wish I could see that America!" said Nikias.

"Oh, you will," Paolos answered, cheerfully. "Everybody does in time." He cleared his throat and said, "Have you ever been anywhere outside the village, Nikias?"

"No," said Nikias, "except up this mountain."

"Oh!" said Paolos. "Well!" And he looked very mysterious. Should he tell Nikias yet about the secret, or should he wait? Perhaps he had better wait.

Soon they came to the high slopes, and there was Demetrios leaning on his staff, watching the sheep. Presently they were all four sitting in the shade of the ailanthus tree, and Nikias was begging:

"That story you said you were saving! Please tell it, Demetrios."

"But who will watch the sheep?" Demetrios asked.

"Oh, but Papous says that the shepherd is his own fence," said Nikias. "See, we are sitting quiet as mice. Please to start."

So Demetrios began this story:

"There was once a great man of Greece called Daedalus. He was as skillful with his tools as Kyr Mihale is with his lesson books, but because he disobeyed a certain king, he was shut away on an island with his son. The king's sailors kept so close a watch that he was unable to escape, try as he would. Then one day Daedalus said to himself:

" 'Even if the king owns the land and the sea, he does not own the air. That way I shall escape.'

"So he started to make a pair of wings for himself and his young son, Icarus, thinking they would both fly away. He put a great many feathers together, beginning with little ones, and adding bigger. The little ones he put together with wax, but for the larger ones he used needle and thread.

And he made the wings in the shape of a bird's wings, curved as they are.

"Little Icarus helped as he could, picking up the feathers that fell, and smoothing out the wax. But most often he was just in the way, because, like most boys, he liked best to play. When Daedalus was finished, he tried out his own wings, and lo and behold, he could fly. Then, just the way a mother bird teaches her fledglings, Daedalus taught Icarus how to trust his wings in the air. So at last the great day came when they were to make their escape.

" 'Icarus,' said Daedalus, 'be sure to keep at a middling height, for if you fly too low the damp air will wet your feathers, and if you fly too high the great heat of the sun will melt them. And hark you, my son, always keep close to me.'

"Then he kissed the little boy and they flew off into the bright sky. What a thrilling flight was that, my Nikias! The shepherds on the hills stopped to gaze up in awe—as you and I did the day we saw the aeroplano—and the plowmen forgot to plow for looking at this miracle. So they flew on, and on. But after a while, Icarus found this flying so pleasant a task that he thought he would fly right up into heaven and pay a visit to the angels. He forgot, you see, to obey his father. Up, up, he flew, until he was higher than any eagle had ever gone. And then the hot sunbeams found him. They began to melt the wax, and the feathers fell one after the other. Then, too late, Icarus, poor lad, remembered and was afraid. He fluttered his arms, but there were no feathers left to hold him. He began to fall, crying loudly for his father. But Daedalus could not hear him, and so Icarus fell right into the sea and was drowned. His father found only the feathers floating on the water, and he grieved a great deal. But the people of Greece never forgot the deed of the little boy. After all, had he not been brave, and have not all of us at one time or another wished to pay a visit to the angels? There was a great sea named after Icarus, and to this day he is remembered."

Demetrios stopped. He yawned and gave a great stretch and whistled to his dog.

"See now," he said, "I have told you the story of the first birdman in history, my Nikias."

Nikias had been sitting there hugging his knees and hardly moving. Even Penelope was still.

"Demetrios." It was Nikias speaking. "Those men who built Paolos' aeroplanos, did they learn the way from Daedalus and Icarus?"

"Some have said so. My father told me it is the first mention of an aeroplano in the story of men."

"At least it would save us a whole lot of time," said Paolos, laughing, "if we could stick them together with wax or a needle."

Nikias lay back, clasping his hands behind his head.

"Perseus, Icarus, and Paolos, they can all fly," he said.

"And who can say," said Demetrios, "but Nikias may be next? On the lap of the god it lies. Well, the thing to remember, my little one, is that a wise boy remembers to obey orders before he tries to show the angels his aeroplano. Is it not so, Paolos?"

"In our country," said Paolos, "we would call that sound advice."

Chapter Fifteen

THE little train went puffing around a bend, saw a yellow river with cypress trees growing beside it, and seemed to make up its mind to find out more about it, because it settled down to follow it. Inside the train on a red plush seat sat Nikias. He was clutching his fez in one hand and a bunch of marjoram herbs in the other, and was sitting up very straight. Beside him, lolling back as if riding on a train were as everyday a matter as eating his supper, was Paolos. Every few minutes Nikias would blink his eyes to see whether he was dreaming. It seemed to him ever since early this morning when Manitza had sprinkled the drops of olive oil on the doorsill to make sure the travelers would have a safe trip, that he, Nikias, *must* be asleep. Paolos was taking him on his first trip on a train, to see the Hanging Monasteries; this was the secret Paolos had been carrying with him for days. Penelope had cried a little because she couldn't go, too, but Papous had said that women were never allowed to visit the Monasteries, so Paolos had promised her a present and Penelope had stopped crying.

After a long ride to a village bigger than his own, there was the big black engine waiting, with white smoke coming from it, and a whistle making a queer exciting sound inside it. And there was the coach with the seats all set next to the widows. By the time he took his seat, Nikias was so full of strange sights that he could hardly do anything but shake his head and give little hoarse squeaks. Hadn't Paolos shown him his first telephone in that village? And let him listen to something that the goblins must have bewitched, because beautiful music was coming right out of a brown box? Paolos laughed and said it was a radio, and there were thousands of them over in America, but Nikias just stood quite still, holding Paolos' sleeve and listening with his eyes popping.

Now they were passing a great snow-capped mountain, and Paolos said it was Mount Olympus, and that Kyr Mihale had told him that they took from it something called asbestos. This was stuff that fire could not hurt. There was a tale that the three men in the Bible story whom Neb-uchadnezzar threw into the fiery furnace had got away alive because they had on asbestos clothes. Thousands of years ago, Paolos said, Greek men and women had woven cloth from these queer threads of rock, while today the as-bestos was used for the brakes of automobiles and firemen's tools.

Nikias listened and watched and now and then asked questions. The train went flying past vineyards and olive fields, rocky slopes and valleys set out in grain; past crum-bling ruins among the tall cypress trees; past little villages and a few big towns. Paolos opened the paper of bread and cheese and almond cakes that Manitza had packed for them, and they ate. The sun was high in the blue sky by now, and it grew very hot, and then the conductor called out some-thing, and they were stepping off the train onto a little wooden platform.

The name of the town was Kalabaka. It was built straight up against the front of a great stone cliff. The little shops and houses seemed to lean right against the mountainside. There were men and boys calling out things for sale. An old man with a thin, cracked voice was selling mulberry leaves, and others, pitchers and fresh fruits. A boy pointed to Nikias' shoes and Paolos laughed and said he was a shoe-shine. Nikias did not know what that was. They went into a coffee shop, and Paolos ordered coffee for himself and milk and stew for Nikias. The owner began to talk with Paolos about the weather, the state of the crops, and about whether there would be war. At last he waddled off to bring the food.

"They are short on hurry, and long on talk in Greece," Paolos said with a laugh.

But Nikias did not mind; Paolos said it as if he loved Greece, too. Anyway, Nikias was busy thinking about other things.

"Paolos," he said, "I should have brought my winged sandals so as I could climb the mountain."

"We'll need your sandals, I'm thinking, and an aeroplano into the bargain," Paolos answered. "That mountain doesn't look like any ant hill."

"I wish Demetrios were here," Nikias said. "It is the only longing I have. Once he told us about the Monasteries."

"Yes, and I asked him all about them after you told me; it was his story that brought me here. Well, we'd better start, old fellow; we've a job cut out, I'm thinking."

They walked down the winding street. Old men were sitting smoking, playing cards, and talking under the sycamore trees. The sidewalks were so narrow that two people had to elbow each other when they passed. Inside his tiny shop almost on the street, a cobbler was squatting; he was stitching busily on a curved-toe shoe, nodding to friends, calling greetings. It was very hot. There were a great many flies; dogs were barking and asses braying, but nobody seemed to mind. Women were drawing water from the spigots in the square, laughing and chattering.

"Look down there," Paolos said, pointing to a queer old

closed carriage. "Once upon a time the Turks used those to drive their families in. The families weren't allowed to see or be seen. Well, it wouldn't have suited *me;* would it you, Nikias?"

"No," answered Nikias. "Papous says my great-grandfather fought those Turks because they wished to make us slaves. It is very unpleasant to be a slave."

"You bet," Paolos said. "Well, what say we forget them? We're supposed to be on an adventure, aren't we?"

"You bet," Nikias said, speaking the first American words he had ever spoken.

Paolos roared with delight.

Soon they came to the foot of the mountain, and the climb began. The trail seemed almost straight up and down. It was so narrow Nikias thought it couldn't have been more than two feet wide. They walked single file. In places there were rough steps cut out of the solid rocks. The path was in the shape of a **U**, and presently turned in between great towering black boulders. It grew almost as dark as night. Nikias could hear Paolos calling anxiously to him, afraid he would slip. But Nikias was as sure-footed as any mountain goat. Paolos did not need to worry about him.

They climbed and climbed, stopping every now and then to catch their breath. Nikias, who had the bright eyes of a country boy, pointed out the swallows' nests in the rocks. After a while they came to their first stop. It was a little place called Aghia Triada, and here Nikias and Paolos saw a queer sight. There was a big net attached to a steel cable,

and inside the net were kindling wood, boxes of food, and a jar of water. They could hear, from high overhead, a faint, rusty, whirring sound; the net was slowly going up.

"A monk away up there," Paolos said, "is pulling up the net."

"But how is he pulling it?" Nikias asked.

"He is walking slowly around a windlass. There are poles in it, and he is pushing them. That's the way the monks get their supplies. Until that iron ladder over there was built, they used to haul up all their *visitors* as well."

"Suppose it broke," Nikias said, staring at the big net.

"Yes, just suppose! *I* prefer my own two good legs. That trolley doesn't look any too strong to me; it has probably rusted with the weather."

They started to climb the iron rungs of the ladder. After a while they came to some more rocky steps that looked as if a giant had cut them. Then they stopped at an iron door jammed into the solid rock. Paolos pulled at a knob, and after a minute they heard the soft tinkling of a bell from above. Someone seemed to press a buzzer, because the door slowly opened, and Paolos and Nikias began to climb the narrowest path either of them had ever seen. On one side was a great cliff, just like a rock wall, and on the other, a drop into a valley hundreds of feet below.

"It feels as if an *empusor* had put an enchantment on us," Nikias whispered.

"An *empusor*?" said Paolos. "What's that?"

"A fairy who is angry at something. It is a good thing Penelope did not come; she wouldn't have liked it."

"*I* was wondering," said Paolos, "what would happen if we met someone coming the other way. I hope all the monks are busy eating their dinner."

After what seemed like hours they came to the top of the peak, and there, just as if they were hanging right into space, were the famous monasteries. They were built of stone and wood, and had tile roofs. A monk came forward and greeted them, and led them into the nearest building.

This was a chapel. The stone walls had queer carvings; they looked, Nikias thought, just like his and Penelope's drawings, not grown-up work at all; but Paolos pointed out a piece of wood that was carved into beautiful flowers, and said it was fine enough to put in a museum in New York. Nikias saw the eikons and bent his head down to the ground as Manitza had told him to.

"Now I will show you the grotto where the remains of the holy St. Stephen lie," the monk said.

They crossed on a dizzy little bridge over a great gorge, and came to a locked door cut out of rock. The monk opened it and there, in a silver sphere, was the skull of St. Stephen. There was a small hole on top of the sphere, and the monk knelt and kissed the head inside. Nikias did this, too; he knew Manitza would like it.

"What are those queer wooden things?" Paolos asked the monk.

"Why, they are eyes and legs and hands," Nikias exclaimed.

"Those have been given to the Monastery," said the monk, "by pilgrims who have been cured of their ills by coming here. You see, they were miracles. The rheumatism in their hands, their crippled legs, or their unseeing eyes were cured, so they thanked God with these gifts."

For a minute nobody spoke. Then the monk led the way back to one of the biggest buildings. They went into a room that had hardly anything in it—no furniture at all except rugs or benches to sleep on. Evidently the monks ate on the floor. A circle of stones had charcoal burning on it, and a big pot of coffee hanging on a tripod. On another queer stone stove what seemed from the smell to be a stew was cooking. There was no chimney, and Nikias wondered where the smoke went to; he supposed it must be through the crevices in the rocks.

Some monks were reading in the room, and others were cooking. The head monk, called the Pater, asked Nikias and Paolos to share their food, and presently they were sitting on the floor and eating a stew made of corn and bread. When Paolos made a funny face over the taste of the milky licorice drink, one of the monks brought him coffee. The monks were very friendly, and asked Paolos all sorts of questions about what was happening in the outside world. Did he think there would be a war in Greece? All the news the monks had was late; the newspaper from Athens was ten days old. Paolos said he hoped there would be no war. Ni-

kias did not say anything; he just sat there eating, and staring around him. What things he would have to tell Manitza!

"Why did they build these monasteries?" Paolos asked the Pater.

"Because men wished to be undisturbed to praise their God," the Pater said. "Some of our brethren sold all their goods and gave the money to the church; some still cultivate their vineyards or watch their sheepfolds down in the valley."

"What, they go up and down those steps every day!" Paolos exclaimed.

"That is nothing," the Pater said quietly.

Paolos laughed. "I've changed my mind," he said. "If

I had to do that often, rather than climb I'd trust my old hide to the net, and be *wound* up."

The Pater smiled.

"But you are American," he said, as if that explained everything.

Then the Pater got up, and led the way out to a sort of balcony with a low railing.

"You may see Greece from here," he said. "Now I must leave you for a while to take my noon rest."

Nikias and Paolos stood there alone on the balcony, looking down. It was a strange and wonderful feeling.

"Look, there is Kalabaka," Paolos said, pointing.

"It looks like Penelope's doll house," Nikias said. "It is so small."

"That is the valley of Peneus over there," Paolos said. "How sandy and yellow it looks; there is not much grass in Greece. Over yonder is the country of Yugoslavia. And, see that river! It is just a tiny stream, but remember, Demetrios told us it is a great torrent in winter."

"Where is the river going?" Nikias asked.

"Through the Vale of Tempe, one of the most beautiful places in all Greece, and at last into the Gulf of Salonika."

"And there what does it do?" Nikias said.

"There it stops being a river and is nothing but some drops of water running into the great sea."

"There are ravens croaking," Nikias cried. "And, listen, I can hear the tinkle of the mules' bells!"

"Whew, think of the monks who built these monasteries!" Paolos said. "Did *they* have courage! You'd think they'd have to be spiders to build walls hanging right over space."

"Yes," said Nikias, "but I'll warrant Perseus or Icarus could have done it. It would have been as easy as *easy* for them."

"It would?" Paolos had his head cocked on one side.

"Perseus would just give his sandals a little push, and Icarus, he would shake out those wings." Nikias looked out of the corner of his eye to see whether Paolos was laughing, but he wasn't.

"Now, if *I* lived up there," Paolos said, "I'd have a moving staircase."

"You are saying a joke, *I bet!*" Nikias said.

But Paolos shook his head as he smiled.

"When you make that trip to New York one of these days, I'll show you I'm not joking," he said. He whistled softly. "If I could only put this view right in my pocketbook and take it back home. My mother and father would call it the finest present I could give them." Paolos stretched out his arms, and filled his lungs with the clear air. "Well, lad," he said, "there's a long dark climb ahead of us, and the sun will be going down before we know it."

"I promised Manitza," said Nikias, "to bring back a small piece of the Pater's robe. She said it would bring her good luck when the bread refuses to rise."

"Come, now, do we snip off a shred when the Pater isn't looking?"

"Oh, no, Manitza said he keeps a special one that people may cut," Nikias said.

Next morning the beautiful, shining motorcar that Paolos had hired drove them along the mountain road that led into the village. They came to a bend, and there it lay, ringed in its snow-peaked mountains. Nikias couldn't understand the way he felt; why, he was *glad* to be home! There he had been on the most exciting trip of his whole life; had seen things that he didn't even know were in the world, and yet the best thing of all was being back home. Why, he must have *missed* the village, and had never known it until this very minute. All of a sudden, Nikias felt that he couldn't wait a minute to get out of that car. Home—it was the very best place on earth. Nikias thought of Demetrios up on the mountain slope sewing on his cowhide sandals, telling the time by the stars, of little Penelope singing to her doll, of Papous' voice whistling to the black mule, and of Manitza saying good night, tucking him into his blankets. The car had hardly come to a stop before Nikias was throwing open the door, running up the path to the cottage. And there, sitting under the plane tree before her loom, was the little bent figure of Manitza.

Nikias gave a shout, and Manitza looked up, letting the bright-colored bobbins that were sliding in and out of the warp fall to the ground.

"Nikias, Nikias," she cried. "May the blessed Virgin be praised, you are safe home!"

And there was Nikias in Manitza's arms, with the breath almost hugged out of his body.

Chapter Sixteen

THE summer passed. Every morning when the cheeping of the swallows woke Nikias and Penelope, he would nudge his sister and whisper: "Paolos, is he *really* here?" And Penelope would laugh merrily and poke him in the ribs, saying, "Wake up, sleepy one. Of course he is here."

One day they would go on a picnic; another, up the mountainside to visit Demetrios and Thalia; on a third, Kyr Mihale would show Paolos the flowers and queer old rocks near the pass. One of the merriest days was the one when they all went to pick grapes, and saw the pretty blue fruit being dried on a terrace to make winter raisins, or trodden out by men's bare feet for wine. Then there had been a merry meal carried from the village by the women, and dancing until the stars came out.

And so the time of the crocuses, hyacinths, and poppies passed, and the lilies and roses came.

Paolos seemed quite happy, learning about his father's country, listening to the tales of old Greece, sitting by Papous in the coffee shop, hearing the travelers talk about the affairs of the great world.

That summer just two things worried the villagers:

When would it rain? And would there be a war? There had not been rain for many weeks, and the peasants were anxious about their fruit and grain.

One day toward the end of summer, Papous came home looking very grave.

"The wells are almost dry," he said.

"May the holy Virgin help us," said Manitza, looking up from her knitting. "Now what shall we do?"

"The Miller says we must hold the festival of Perperouna," Papous said.

"What is that?" asked Paolos, looking up from the book he was reading in the pleasant shade of the big plane tree.

"A custom of our country when there is a drought," Manitza said. "A girl is chosen to be Perperouna; there are prayers and songs and a parade."

"Oh, who will be Perperouna?" asked Penelope, eagerly.

"The Miller suggests that you be chosen, my child," Papous said, gravely. "Always a girl-child without mother or father is taken, because the good God is more apt to have pity on her prayer."

"Oh, Papous," cried Penelope, jumping up and down and clapping her hands. "How happy I am! I shall wear the beautiful dress of leaves and the crown of flowers, and everyone will look at me."

Manitza laid her hand on Penelope's arm.

"You forget," she said gravely, "that Perperouna must be a child without a wicked thought or selfish wish. Otherwise why should God listen to her prayer?"

"Perperouna must sing the song, and make the prayer that will knock at God's door," Papous said, gently.

Penelope had tears in her eyes.

"Oh, I'll be good! I'll be good!" she cried.

"But of course! Our little maid will be the best Perperouna in Greece," Paolos said. "She's sweet and pretty enough to bring down rain on a sunny day."

Right next morning the festival was held, for everyone was too worried to risk putting it off. All the children met in the woods outside the village. A vote was taken and sure enough Penelope was chosen for the part of Perperouna. It was just as if she were going to be in that Christmas play that Kyr Mihale had written, Nikias thought; just as if she were going to have the leading part in it. He felt very proud as he saw Penelope being led away by the Miller's wife, Thalia, and Manitza. He knew they would strip her of her everyday clothes, and she would be dressed in a tunic of leaves, with a crown of roses on her head.

Nikias felt a little worried, too. What would happen to the figs and melons and plums, all the wheat that Manitza made into *trahana,* if no rain came? It is a good thing that a boy is not chosen, Nikias thought, because it might have been me, and probably God wouldn't listen to me when it is anything important like this.

Then the trees and shrubs parted, and there was Penelope dressed in her pretty flowery costume, her eyes shining, her cheeks very rosy. All the other children fell into line be-

hind her, the Pappas said a prayer, and the parade moved
down into the village, singing this song as they marched:

"Perperouna makes this prayer,
    Going on her way:
    'To grow the corn and cotton fair,
    Send us rain today.
    For herbs to sprout and buds to flower,
    Take away their thirst;
    Make the world a happy bower;
    Let the dry springs burst.' "

As the procession passed along the streets, they stopped
and knocked on the cottage doors. Then the owner of the
place came out and sprinkled Perperouna with a few drops
of water. Nobody laughed, because it was a very grave
thought that the wells might grow dry, and the fruits and
grain thirst. It was nearly dark when the parade was over
and Penelope and Nikias reached home. Penelope was too
tired and excited even to eat, and Manitza put her right to
bed. But late into the night Nikias would wake and see the
figures of Papous and Manitza kneeling before the eikon
praying.

All next day the people of the village watched the skies
with anxious eyes to see if any rain cloud had gathered.
Nikias and Penelope went up the mountain to a high slope
and watched from there. But the hot sky stayed blue and
cloudless. On the second day, though, Nikias and Penelope

woke to feel the air cool, and above their heads they saw heavy black clouds gathering in the east. Papous was kneeling in the doorway, praying. An hour later the rain came. First there was a storm with lightning and thunder; the rain fell so hard that the two children thought the whole world would be drowned. They saw Papous holding a long black-handled knife and making passes in the air. They knew what he was doing; he was cutting the storm. And after a while the storm must have heard him, because it stopped, and there was only the steady sound of rain beating on the tiled roof. The fruits and grain were saved.

"You see," said Penelope, standing beside Nikias and looking out at the downpour, "I can't be so *very* bad. I brought the rain down."

And she laughed and clapped her hands. Nikias felt so happy that he laughed, too, and Paolos caught Penelope up in his arms and whirled her around and around.

"She's the best little Perperouna in the world," he said.

Manitza made a jerking movement of her head.

"It is God who is good," she said.

Chapter Seventeen

SEPTEMBER came and so did harvest time. The land looked as if it were covered with a carpet of bright flowers. There was the crimson cyclamen, a purple bush called osier, and, higher up on the slopes, the purple heather. Paolos tasted the delicious big cucumbers that the Greeks eat when they are thirsty. The crickets whirred and the sky was as blue as an iris.

For days Manitza had been making bread. In the kneading trough outside, she had shaped long loaves of the whole-wheat dough and set them between strips of muslin. Holly branches had been burned in the oven until it was very hot, then the ashes were swept out, and the loaves slid in to bake on wooden shovels.

Now everyone was on the way to the harvest fields. Papous' black mule held in its panniers food and blankets, for they were to spend several nights in the open fields. As they went, other villagers joined them. There were the Miller and his wife, Kyr Mihale, Theo and his father, the shoemaker, and even the priest who, as usual on special occasions, had tucked his long beard into his girdle. The day was so bright and everything looked so shining and clean that Papous could not help calling Paolos' attention to it in a very proud way.

"Is it not beautiful?" he asked.

Paolos smelled the flowers and shrubs; he smiled.

"It sort of gets you," he said. "I'm beginning to feel almost like a Greek myself."

"God grant no enemy comes to spoil the land," Papous said.

"Though my own father was a soldier in the World War," said Paolos, "it is hard to think there is war again in this year of 1940."

Kyr Mihale shook his head to mean yes.

"Soon it may be our turn," he said.

"You look very calm when you talk of war," said Paolos.

"A Greek takes such things as they come," Kyr Mihale answered. "There are always wars going on in this sad world; one must not be afraid if one loses or show great triumph if one wins."

"I don't feel that way," Paolos said. "I think we should work so there will never be any more wars, but all men will be brothers."

And then Nikias pulled at Paolos' sleeve and gave a great shout, for there were Demetrios and Thalia and their fat donkey coming down the mountain trail. Everyone forgot about mere wars. Nikias ran to meet his friends, and there were merry greetings. Demetrios had brought a great fresh cheese in a goatskin, and of course his reed.

"On the soul of my father, I have not seen you for many

132

days," he said to Nikias; "not since we sheared. I vow you would not know the sheepfold; the thyme has gone, but the lentisk berries are red as the roof of your mouth, and every plane tree has a wreath of laurel around it."

"Demetrios, will there be time for a story?" Nikias asked.

Demetrios laughed his friendly laugh.

"Oh, ho, what can a great traveler like you want with my poor tales?" he asked, teasingly. Then he made a grab at Nikias' shirt. "You have a grasshopper inside and it tickles you," he said; "it is the same game I played when I was a lad."

Presently they came to the harvest fields. Others were there, too, men from the mountains who wanted to exchange their labor for a share of the crops. Huts of grass and reed had been built where people could watch to see that the crops were not stolen by outsiders, and every place was decorated with garlands of flowers. The little fields had been sown by hand, and they were cut in the same way; there were no great farm machines. The sheaves were piled high on the backs of the donkeys or into the red wagons. Everyone worked, children as well as grown folks. They sang and laughed and ate in the open. When night came, they gathered around Demetrios and he played on his reed and told them stories.

Next morning when the sheaves were taken to the threshing floor, Nikias and Penelope and Theo rode on top of the Miller's wagon drawn by two sleek oxen. The threshing floor was paved with cobblestones. Every farmer took turns with another on his own pile. The grain was spread a little at a time on the floor, and then two horses were driven around and around until their hoofs had beaten out the chaff and stalks from the kernels. The sun made the floor as hot as an oven, but the patient horses kept on walking. Nikias was glad to remember that after working two or three months, they would be turned loose in the mountains to rest until next year. Nikias was working, too; after the grain had been separated, there was the winnowing to do by hand, and all the children helped in this, tossing the grain into the air with wooden shovels.

When the wheat of Papous, Kyr Mihale, and the Miller was all winnowed, they still stayed on to help their neighbors. Every night the merrymaking grew. There was a dance that Nikias and Penelope loved; it was to the corn spirit and everyone joined in, no matter what his age. Paolos worked and sang and danced with the rest. Everyone knew and liked him now; they forgot he was an American and treated him just as if he were one of them. Every evening there was a little knot of the younger people gathered about him, asking questions about America, and especially about the areoplano he flew.

The night before they were all to leave for home, Nikias sat close beside Demetrios under a big ailanthus tree, a little apart from the others.

"Yesterday I heard Papous tell Kyr Mihale that war comes closer every day," Nikias said.

"Well?" said Demetrios.

"If there is a war, will you fight, Demetrios?"

"What else! Would you not defend your home if a robber came?"

"Yes," said Nikias. "Demetrios, I wish I were a grown man, and could fly an aeroplano. Then, perhaps—I could fight for Greece. Kyr Mihale says it is aeroplanos that our country needs the most."

"Oh, ho, my little warrior," said Demetrios, laughing, "is it not enough for you to fly in your thoughts with Perseus and Icarus?"

There was a bright star twinkling just over their heads; it was quiet out in the field.

"Demetrios," asked Nikias, "do you think Paolos believes I will ever be the sort of boy who—who could fly an aeroplano?"

"What do you think I am? A goblin, that I can peer inside Paolos' head?" Demetrios stopped and put his arm about Nikias' shoulder. He wasn't laughing now. "Do you know the meaning of the word *Nikias,* your own name?" he asked.

"No."

"It means the victor," said Demetrios. "Forget not that, little lad."

Chapter Eighteen

IT WAS a day in early November. In the schoolyard, Theo and some of the other boys were playing soldiers. Penelope was sitting propped up against the trunk of a tree, winding a bandage made from her kerchief about the leg of the doll from America. Greece had gone to war; the enemy had invaded the country. Word had even come that they were dropping bombs on islands and cities near the sea. But it seemed to Nikias that they had done a worse thing than that; they had taken both Paolos and Demetrios away.

Inside the schoolhouse, too worried even to play, Nikias was cleaning off the blackboard. Kyr Mihale had given him the job because he thought it would keep his mind off thoughts of the war. But it had not. Nikias was remembering just two things: Demetrios saying good-by, and Paolos waving from the red wagon.

Demetrios had come walking up the path to Papous' house one afternoon the week before. He carried a bundle over his shoulder, and he was whistling.

"Oh, ho, my Nikias," he called, "where are you hiding?"

Nikias ran out from the back of the house where he was piling fagots of holly wood.

"Here I am, Demetrios," he called happily.

"I but stopped in to let you know," Demetrios said, "that Kyr Mihale or Papous must spin tales for you for a while. I will be busy elsewhere."

"Demetrios," Nikias said, his face going white, "are you—going to war?"

"And where else, little countryman! When there are locusts on your land, do you lie down and let them crawl over your body?"

Nikias threw his arms around Demetrios' waist and buried his face in his sleeve.

"No, no," he cried, "you must not go."

"But that is truly a foolish speech," Demetrios said in a quiet voice. "Did not a soldier in uniform come for me? Did he not tell me they wanted me for scouting duty?"

"What is that?"

"A scouting band goes ahead of the army, finding out about the lay of the land, where the water is, how far the enemy has come. Look, you, is it not a great honor? They have heard that I know so much about these mountain slopes that they trust me to be a scout. On the soul of my father, I am glad now that I trained in the army for two years not so long ago."

"Where will you be, Demetrios?"

"Perhaps not so far away. That I cannot say, though. Reports have it the enemy is marching through the country of Albania, and Albania, as you know, is our next-door neighbor beyond the mountain range."

"What—what shall I do when you're gone, Demetrios?"

"Ho, what shall you do! Be a brave son of Greece, of course. Look, you, when I come back, I shall have so many tales to tell they will take until Christmas time."

That was the first thing Nikias was thinking of now, and the second was the day Paolos left. He was an American, but he had asked to fly an aeroplano for Greece. There were not enough pilots and they had been glad to have him, Papous said. The day he left, Manitza, Penelope, Papous, Kyr Mihale, and Nikias had gone to the square to see him off. Nikias had only a minute or two with him alone.

"Maybe one of these days," Paolos said, patting Nikias' shoulder, "I'll be dropping you a letter right out of the clouds. You want to watch for me."

"Paolos," Nikias said, "don't go away. Demetrios has gone."

"What, don't you want me to be a good soldier of Greece, like Demetrios and Perseus and—who was that other fellow—Icarus?"

"I am lonely without you," Nikias said.

"But I thought Greek boys were brave. Look, if you were over in America you would be playing in a band for me, and calling: 'May Lady Luck ride the beams for you, Paolos.' You wouldn't be crying like that."

"L-lady Luck, who is she?"

"Lady Luck is the same in every land, Nikias, and the beams are what guide an aeroplano safely into port."

And then Paolos had jumped in the wagon, waving his hand gaily, and the red wagon had disappeared around the bend in the road.

Now Nikias' eraser was rubbing and rubbing at the blackboard.

"Come," said Kyr Mihale, "you have wiped the board so clean I shall be ashamed to write another arithmetic lesson on it. Go out in the sun and play with the others."

"Demetrios has sent no word—nor Paolos."

"No news," Kyr Mihale said, "has usually the way of being good news. Look, you! In war they who stay at home must wear the armor of a smile."

"I cannot smile," Nikias answered. "I try, but my face refuses."

"What, are you not the one who would one day fly a great aeroplano?"

"Yes, Kyr Mihale."

"Then, the thing a pilot learns first before he flies is to trust himself."

"How do you trust yourself?"

"You truly wish to know?" Kyr Mihale asked, gently.

"Yes."

"Do the thing you are afraid of, Nikias."

"What thing?" asked Nikias, slowly.

Kyr Mihale began to place crayons on the desks.

"A thing that perhaps will come sooner than you think," he said.

Chapter Nineteen

IT WAS a morning two weeks later. Nikias was wakened by the sound of a voice speaking in a low whisper to Papous. A minute later he heard his grandfather saying his name.

"Make haste and put on your clothes," he said. "Kyr Mihale would speak to you. And, quiet, do not waken your sister."

Nikias, wondering what could have happened, scrambled into his shirt and *fustanella*. He saw that Papous and Kyr

Mihale were sitting under the plane tree now, talking in a low voice. He hurried out.

"Nikias," Kyr Mihale said. He was looking at Nikias with a queer, excited look in his eyes that were usually such quiet, schoolteacher eyes. "Are you willing to do something for your country?"

Nikias could feel his heart thumping.

"Yes, Kyr Mihale," he said.

"Even if there is danger in the doing?"

Nikias dug his bare foot into the leaves so that Kyr Mihale would not see he could not keep it steady.

"Y-yes," he said.

"It is both for Greece and for Demetrios," Kyr Mihale said.

Nikias' ears pricked up.

"Demetrios!" he said. "Is he in danger?"

"Hush, not so loud," Papous said. "This is for your ears alone."

"Come closer," Kyr Mihale said. "We have had word that a Greek regiment is coming to meet the enemy just beyond the mountain. Demetrios has been chosen for the scouting band, the men who go ahead. He and those with him are not more than four miles from here, just beyond Philos Pass."

"Demetrios, he is close?" Nikias asked in so low a voice that Papous and Kyr Mihale could hardly hear him. "What is he doing?"

"He is spying on the enemy. Watching them to see

what way they take through the mountain passes. Then he will run and tell his regiment."

"Demetrios is fleet as a mountain goat," Papous said. "He knows every rock and tree for miles around. No one is like him."

No, no one was like him! Nikias knew that; unless it was Paolos.

"What do you wish me to do?" Nikias said.

"We have reason to think that Demetrios and his men have little fresh food," Kyr Mihale said. "They are a long way from the regiment and its supplies."

"So it is our plan," said Papous, putting his hand on Nikias' arm, "that *you* carry him milk and cheese and fresh baked bread."

"There is but one person in the village who knows these hills almost as well as Demetrios," Kyr Mihale said, watching Nikias, "and that is you, lad."

Nikias could not say a word. He rubbed his tongue over his dry lips.

"If any scouting band of the enemy should be close," Kyr Mihale said, "we think they would not question a child. If it were a grown person, they might stop and ask him where he was going."

Still Nikias did not say anything.

"But we think there is small danger of any enemy," Papous said. "I would not allow you to go if there were."

"You remember our talk at school?" Kyr Mihale asked. He was holding Nikias' hand. "When I told you your country might need you sooner than you thought—when you would find a chance to look your fear in the face? That chance has come. Will you take it, Nikias?"

It did not seem to Nikias that he was talking at all; it seemed like somebody else. But he heard a voice saying:

"I will go."

Kyr Mihale and Papous looked at each other and sighed.

"I thought you would, Nikias," Kyr Mihale said. "You will be ready to start in an hour. You will take the mule. Now, listen, and I will tell you the way."

Then Kyr Mihale began to draw a map with a stick on the ground.

Five hours later Nikias stopped the black mule in a little clearing set between two great mountain peaks. It could go no farther; there was a climb sheer up the side of the farther mountain that Nikias would have to take alone. He lifted the two panniers from the mule's back, patted his head, then strapped the panniers to his own shoulders. In the still, cold air he could smell the cheese and garlic and fresh brown bread. Slowly, carefully, he began to climb.

In places the trail was so steep he had to stop and take deep breaths before he made a leap to some jutting ledge. But he managed it; he knew and loved these mountains well. Had not he and Demetrios looked for eagles' nests and blue lupine flowers here many a time? There! He was almost to the top. The scrub pine was just above his head; he could smell it. He clambered on a few feet, and there he was on top of the ridge. The cold air blew in his face.

It seemed as if he could see a hundred miles or more across the valleys and rocky peaks. Slowly, Nikias got his breath, setting the panniers down on the ground. Demetrios should be here; right here—

Nikias gave a little shout. There, not more than fifty yards away, were four men sitting in a little circle, studying a map. And the man who held the map was Demetrios. Nikias went scrambling down the slope, pulling the panniers by the strap. He went running right into Demetrios' outstretched arms.

"Nikias!" Demetrios cried. He was staring at Nikias as if he were a ghost. "What are you doing here?"

"Demetrios," Nikias said, "you are alive—well?"

"But, of course."

"I have brought you food, Demetrios. See, here in the baskets—bread that Manitza has baked, and mincemeat. And here are cheese and garlic."

Demetrios looked at the other men. His voice sounded quite stern.

"How did you know where we were?" he asked.

"Kyr Mihale and Papous, they sent me; I don't know how they knew. Demetrios, where is your uniform?"

"Papous and Kyr Mihale! Then it is well," Demetrios said. Now he was smiling. "My uniform? I do not wear one. Now I must introduce you; men, this is my friend. Nikias."

Nikias made a bow to the three men.

"Well," said one of them, a young man with very

146

white teeth and a pleasant smile. "This Nikias, he is a guest from heaven! My poor mouth waters at the thought of that mincemeat."

"Nikias," Demetrios said, "you have seen Thalia? She is well?"

"Yes," said Nikias, "but I think perhaps she misses you."

The young soldier laughed.

"Miss that old mountain goat!" he said. "All he thinks of is what ilex tree the enemy will pass at six o'clock tomorrow morning; what rock they will sit on the day after at high sun. Hark, you, comrade, will you open those baskets, or must I do it for you? Do you not see that I perish?"

Demetrios began slowly to open one of the baskets, while the other men crowded around him, laughing, talking.

"Nikias," Demetrios said, "you must never tell anyone where we are. You promise?"

"I promise," Nikias said. "No one knows I am here except Manitza, Papous, and Kyr Mihale."

"Then I say no more. You are as welcome as the flowers in May, my Nikias." Demetrios laughed. "Come, you greedy vultures, dip your beaks into this bread."

Chapter Twenty

I T WAS a bright cold morning near the end of November. Nikias was leading the little black mule along the mountain trail. When its feet slipped on the pebbles, Nikias would reach over and steady the baskets. He was on his way to Demetrios with food. For three weeks now he had been carrying him bread, cheese, garlic, and Manitza's cookies. By now he knew every stick and stone of the way.

Nikias was whistling softly to himself. He felt happy and not at all worried. Not once had he met a stranger. Hadn't Kyr Mihale such trust in him as a messenger that he even excused him from his lessons? Of course, Penelope and Theo and the other boys and girls wondered, but when they asked him Nikias always said, "I cannot say."

Nikias had just come to the steep slope that led to the clearing, when he heard his name called. The sound seemed to come from close behind him. He spun around, and there were Penelope and Theo. They must have followed him. Nikias did not speak. He stood still, frowning.

"Why did you do this, Penelope?" he said at last. "Kyr Mihale and Papous will be very angry."

Penelope shuffled her foot in the pebbly trail, but Theo made a rude face.

"Aha, so the mountains are not free!" he said. "They belong only to Nikias, the great Perseus."

"Why are you not at school, Theo?" Nikias asked. "What will Kyr Mihale say?"

"Oh, Nikias," Penelope begged, "please, don't scold us. You see, the other night I—I heard Manitza and Papous talking. They thought I was asleep, but I wasn't. I heard them say you were bringing food to Demetrios."

"So you told Theo?" Nikias asked.

"She had to tell me," Theo said in a bragging voice. "She was afraid to follow you unless I brought her. She knew that I, Theo, am not afraid of anyone—even of the enemy."

"It was a wicked thing to do, Penelope," Nikias said.

"Oh, ho, so *you* are the only boy in the village who is good enough to carry food to our soldiers!" Theo stood with his feet wide apart, his chin stuck out. "Well, you will find you are mistaken. From now on Theo Porto, the shoemaker's son, will carry to the troops bread and mince-meat that *his* mother has made."

"Nikias," Penelope said, her lip trembling, "I—I told Thalia because I thought she would want to send a message to Demetrios. And she wrote a letter, and I have it here, with a package of sweetmeats. You—you would not want Demetrios not to see Thalia's letter, Nikias?"

Nikias leaned his head against the rocky wall that lined

one side of the trail. He did not know what to do. Of course, Penelope, and Theo, too, were all right; they would not want any harm to come to the regiment. They just did not know how important a job this was. And besides, would not Demetrios be happy to have that letter of Thalia's? To know that all was well with the sheepfold, and that she was in good health? But what would Kyr Mihale say if he knew Penelope and Theo had followed him? What was it Demetrios had said Icarus should have done? *Obeyed orders and used his head!* Kyr Mihale had trusted him, Nikias; he couldn't disappoint him. Suppose —suppose he let them come just as far as the clearing, and then told them to go back with the black mule? Penelope could never climb that steep trail. If Theo refused to turn back, he, Nikias, wouldn't move a step farther. He would just sit there, if it took *all night,* and not say a word about where he was going until they *had* to go back. Penelope would be afraid when the darkness came, and besides she would think about how Manitza would punish her. Manitza had a switch.

"I will let you come as far as the clearing," Nikias said. His voice did not sound as it usually did; it was just like Kyr Mihale's.

"Perhaps Perseus will soon tie on his winged sandals," Theo said. "Perhaps he will drop the bread and garlic to Demetrios from a cloud."

"But when we get there, you must turn back," Nikias said.

150

"Oh, ho, we must! Well, I'll tell you; Demetrios will soon see there are other warriors in the village besides this Nikias," Theo said.

"Come on," Nikias said.

Penelope did not say anything; she was looking out of the corner of her eye at Nikias. He looked very stern; he did not look at all like himself. The little black mule began to pick its way carefully down the trail, and the children followed.

Presently they came to the ravine. Nikias was just easing the mule down the slope, making a little coaxing sound with his lips, when there came a tiny sharp rattle of stones. All three of them stood quite still. There was a second trail down the slope, and along it was coming a party of six men, dressed in a strange uniform. They were scrambling down one after the other and a tall man in front was waving to the children.

Nikias thought he must be dead. His heart had stopped beating; he couldn't feel it at all. *He knew who those men were!* He had seen a picture of them in the paper Kyr Mihale had from Athens. They were soldiers of the enemy! He could not speak. He felt Penelope's fingers digging into his arm. He heard Theo's breath coming in choking sounds. *They* knew, too.

"Nikias," Theo whispered, "they—they—"

"Yes," Nikias said. It did not seem as if his lips could move; they were stiff.

151

"Oh, Nikias," said Penelope, beginning to cry, "I am afraid."

Demetrios had to have that food! He would be expecting it. Had not Kyr Mihale said they *might* see the enemy, and they would not harm children? Well, he, Nikias, was the messenger, was he not? He would *have* to do something.

"Hark, you," Nikias said, quickly, "if they ask us anything, we must pretend that we know nothing. We—we go on a picnic."

The man in the lead was shouting something now. He was beckoning to them to wait.

"They'll kill us," Penelope whispered.

"No," Nikias said. "Just—just leave it to me."

Now the men were beside them. They were very smart in their dark uniforms, with braid and buttons, and they carried revolvers in their belts. The man in the lead was smiling, but it did not seem like a real smile.

"A good year to you, my lad," he said to Nikias. He spoke in Greek.

"A—a good year to you, master," Nikias said, hoarsely.

"Your face is white; you are sick?" the man said.

"Perhaps one of their goblins has stolen his tongue." It was another soldier speaking. He had queer, angry black eyes; he was not smiling.

"I—we go on a picnic," Nikias said. "We—we eat over yonder near that stream."

152

"Oh, ho, a picnic," said the first man. "Maybe we can add something to that."

"Maybe we can," said the second man. His eyes did not look as if they ever blinked.

"Look——" it was the first man speaking again—— "here is a package of sweetmeats. I have been saving it for just such a pretty little maid as that one there. On my soul, I even think there is enough for all three."

Nikias knew that when anyone offered you food it was to befriend you, and you must take it for politeness' sake. Had not Manitza told him that a dozen times? Penelope was not saying anything. She was pressed up close against Nikias, her hands over her eyes. Theo was looking at the ground; he was not moving at all.

"I thank you," said Nikias, holding out his hand for the sweetmeats.

"Ho, the cockerel gets more friendly," said the second man, "but the little hen hides under her feathers. Perhaps, Benito, the children of these mountains have no tongues."

"Peace, Rafael," the first man said; he was frowning. "I can handle them."

"May——may the holy Virgin bless you," Nikias said. He pretended to bite into one of the sweetmeats.

"Ah, that is better," said the first man. He was smiling again. "Now, hark you, will you do a small thing in return for our gift?" He was looking at Nikias. "Come, what is your name?" he asked. "You listen, but you do not hear. Of what are you afraid?"

"I—I am afraid of nothing," Nikias said. "The sweet-meats, they are very good."

How far away were Demetrios and the others? Were they close? Would they—would they come climbing down that trail over there, and the enemy catch them? *I have to say something,* Nikias thought!

"What would you have us do?" he said.

The first man stood curling the ends of his black mustache.

"Oh, it is nothing," he said. "We are looking for a band of soldiers. We—we wish to give them a friendly message. On your way here, did you see any such?"

Holy Virgin, help me, Nikias thought. What were those words? *Obey orders, and keep your head.*

"Yes, we saw them," Nikias said. He was speaking in a whisper you could hardly hear. "They—they were not dressed as you are."

"Which way did they go?" the first man said. Suddenly his voice was frightening; he was not smiling at all.

Nikias pointed up the path they had come.

"We met them perhaps a quarter-mile back," he said. "They were headed toward the west."

Demetrios' hiding place was straight *east,* over the ridge.

The first man came very close. Nikias could feel his breath. His arm hurt where the man held it.

"You would not lie, cockerel?" he said.

"No," Nikias said.

The man said something to the others in a speech Nikias

did not understand, then without a word he turned toward the trail that Nikias and the others had just traveled. He began to climb, the others behind him.

Nobody spoke for a minute; they were watching the men disappear around the bend. Then Theo said:

"That was a lie you told, Nikias."

"Yes," Nikias said.

"It was to save Demetrios," Penelope said. She looked whiter than the sheets at home. "They would have—have killed him if they knew where he was."

"Yes," Nikias said.

"What shall we do now?" Penelope said. She was pressing still closer to Nikias.

"Nikias," Theo said, speaking in a whisper. "When they find out you lied, they will—come back. They will—kill us, Nikias."

Nikias did not say anything for a minute. Theo was right, but a queer thing was happening inside Nikias. It was just as if he were listening to a story Demetrios was telling, and he knew, without being told, what the end was going to be! Those soldiers would be coming back soon; they would guess that Demetrios and the others were very close. They would come back, and take the only other trail—the one up the mountain. And they would creep up on Demetrios and kill him and the others. The story, it had to end one way: *he must climb that mountain and warn Demetrios!*

"Theo," he said, "you and Penelope go back to the village. You know that path to the north; it branches off from the main trail. It is near the two tall balsams; you must watch for it. That way you will not meet the enemy. Tell Kyr Mihale what has happened. You must go right away, Theo."

"But what will you do?" Penelope said, staring at Nikias.

It seemed to Nikias that he could hear Manitza's voice calling him to supper, could see Papous smiling at him across the hearthstone, could hear the sleepy twittering of the swallows in the eaves. Nikias looked up the dark wall of the mountain, and he felt afraid—more afraid than he had ever felt before in all his life. And then suddenly he felt angry at those soldiers who were looking for Demetrios, and he did not feel afraid at all.

"I will climb the peak to warn Demetrios," he said.

"But they'll come back after you, Nikias," Theo said.

And Nikias remembered something else.

"A regiment sends a scouting band ahead when—when it is near something," he said.

"You mean—" began Theo, and stopped.

"I mean our regiment must be close. Those soldiers were looking for *it*."

"And the enemy has a regiment, too?" Theo whispered. He was edging along toward the trail.

"It may be close," Nikias said.

Then he started to run. He did not even wait to see Penelope and Theo go scrambling back up the trail. Nikias set his foot on the little slippery ledge that marked the beginning of the path up the mountain. He began to climb. Every now and then he stopped to look back, to catch his breath; but he could see no one coming. Now and then he had to make a wild clutch at a bush or tree root to save himself from falling. He could feel his heart pounding; it felt as if it would come straight through his shirt. He clambered on. It seemed as if an hour had passed. Now he could see the top of the peak. It was not more than six feet above him. But there seemed no hold right there. He reached out toward a sharp jutting boulder; he thought he could swing himself up to it. But the rock was slippery, and besides his hands were wet with perspiration. His fingers closed about air—he heard himself scream—he felt himself fall.

It must have been a fall of perhaps eight feet; then he struck a ledge of rocky soil. It and the panniers broke his fall, but his body hit very hard. For a moment he lay there trying to breathe, wondering whether he was alive. And then a pain like a red-hot needle went tearing along his shoulder bone. He closed his eyes and lay still. Demetrios was up there, expecting him, waiting for him, hungry perhaps. And he had failed him. Demetrios, and perhaps—perhaps the regiment, too! Perseus did not stop when the sea monster struck. He was bleeding with a dozen wounds, but he thrust back again. Perseus was trying to save Andromeda, a girl; he, Nikias, must save *Demetrios and a regiment!*

Nikias pulled himself up on his good arm. See, there

was a firm-looking ledge just above. He could reach it if he tried hard. The pain in his left shoulder blade felt like a blazing fire in his flesh. Well, but *Demetrios was waiting!* Nikias' hand closed about the rock. With an effort that seemed to wrench every inch of his body, he pulled himself up. Two feet, three feet, four! There, just above his head were the scrub pine and the juniper bushes that marked the top. Nikias made a tiny whimpering sound that was like a puppy's, and pulled himself over the top.

He lay quite still then. He felt as if he would never move again. His shoulder was a great lump of pain. Things were going dark before his eyes. He—he was falling asleep. But Demetrios was waiting up here; he must not sleep. He gave a little shout, and waited, but no one answered. And suddenly Nikias remembered the call Demetrios made to the sheep. Demetrios could hear that sound; he could hear it a quarter of a mile away. Nikias twisted his lips and called the sheep call.

Ten minutes later when Demetrios knelt beside him, anxiously whispering his name, rubbing his hands, Nikias moved. He had fainted, but he did not know it. He thought he had just fallen asleep. He felt as if he had been to some place a long way away. He opened his eyes, and there was Demetrios kneeling beside him, calling his name.

"Demetrios," Nikias whispered, "the food is all spoiled, but I had to let you know—the enemy—they have a scouting band—down below. They're looking for you. They asked us where you were. I—I told them you had gone west. They will know I have lied, and come back. They will—will bring their regiment around the **U** trail below the pass. Demetrios, I—I—"

And then Nikias fainted again.

Chapter Twenty-one

I T WAS dark when Penelope and Theo reached home. Penelope was limping and crying, but Theo was not saying anything at all. His lips were closed tight. Only when he found Kyr Mihale at Nikias' house did he tell his tale. When he was through, Manitza knelt and prayed before the eikon, but Papous went to the door and looked out into the black night. Kyr Mihale put his arm around Papous' shoulder.

"There is nothing we can do tonight," he said. "The holy Virgin will watch over the boy."

"I pray God!" said Papous.

"Is he not on an errand for his country, my friend?"

"There is fresh snow on the pass," Papous said. "The trails are dangerous."

"But Nikias knows them in his sleep."

"The enemy, it may be close."

"And *our* regiment, it may be close, too."

"What will happen?" Papous whispered.

"God knows," Kyr Mihale said. "Look you, Kyr Yannio, if there is no news of Nikias by tomorrow morning, the Miller and I will set out to find him. Now I must go home and sleep so that I will be in readiness."

161

Kyr Mihale was halfway down the path when he heard Theo's voice close behind him.

"I must speak to you," Theo said.

"The night grows late. What is it, Theo?"

"It is only this: *I* am the coward, not Nikias."

"I could have told you that before this," Kyr Mihale said. "Courage does not live only on the wrestling mat."

"When Nikias went up the mountain to warn them, *I* ran home."

"But he bade you go, did he not?" Kyr Mihale's voice was gentler.

"Yes, and there was Penelope to care for. But, Kyr Mihale, there is more. I laughed at Nikias with the others; I mocked at him for a coward. That time he wore the mask of Perseus—"

Kyr Mihale saw that Theo was crying.

"There is but one thing that will give you peace to-night," he said, "and that is to confess your sin to the Pappas. He may have gone to bed, but I think we can rouse him."

The Pappas was sitting reading a book of Aesop's Fables when they knocked, liking to do this just before he slept. He listened to their tale without speaking. When they were through, he nodded gravely, said good night to Kyr Mihale, and took Theo out the door and across the garden that led to the church.

Inside a little room there was a table. On each side was a bench, so close to the table that one had to slide into it in

162

a sitting position. There was no way for Theo to get out unless the Pappas opened the door. Pappas began to speak in a low, grave voice.

Meanwhile at home, Penelope was kneeling before the eikon. The little lamp beneath it was burning brightly to show that Christ is the light of the world. Penelope was praying, and sobbing as she prayed. She was a disobedient girl; she had followed Nikias when she knew it was forbidden. She was vain, too; always thinking of her aprons or her kerchiefs, washing off the soot from behind her ear after Manitza had put it there. Now her wickedness might mean that Nikias would never come back any more. The enemy—it might find him and carry him away to that country beyond the great sea. Penelope prayed to be forgiven.

When she had finished her prayer, Manitza did not say anything to her, and Penelope crept into bed to cry into her pillow. It was the first time in her life that Manitza had not said good night.

Chapter Twenty-two

WHEN Nikias opened his eyes the second time, he was lying inside a tent on an army cot. He moved his shoulder cautiously, and then he saw that his shirt had been taken off and his shoulder was bandaged. There was a funny smell to it, too. But it did not hurt the way it had. He wondered where he was. He was not at home; he could see that. He called Demetrios' name, and a minute later Demetrios opened the canvas flap and came in. He was smiling. His teeth looked very white in his tanned skin.

"Oh, ho, little Icarus!" he said. "So you try to fly up the mountainside."

"Where am I, Demetrios?"

"In our army camp, patriot. All alone with me and Joannes."

"The regiment—is it safe, Demetrios?"

"Aye, thanks to you, Nikias."

"To me?"

"Your warning reached us in time. Luckily the enemy's troops came without aeroplano." Demetrios took Nikias' hand and held it in a tight clasp. "Look, lad, my colonel has told me I may let you into a great secret."

"A secret?"

"From what you told us, we knew where the enemy's men must be, and I remembered that narrow pass beyond the peak that you and I used to call Old Bald Head. Our regiment will cross it. If they reach there in time, they will be able to cut off the enemy's flank—attack them from the rear. It may mean a great victory, Nikias."

"Oh, Demetrios," Nikias whispered. It was all he could say. There were tears squeezing out between his closed eyelids.

"You and I," said Demetrios, "are soldiers of Greece; we do not talk of our deeds. I will but say to you: You are a brave lad, Nikias."

Nikias held his breath.

"*I* am brave, Demetrios!"

"But, yes. You fly now, little lad. Your wings before this were wax like Icarus'; it was only your imagination that flew then. But now they are strong; you fly them in the middle air. It is well."

It seemed to Nikias his heart was thumping so hard Demetrios must hear it!

"Will Paolos think I am brave?" he said.

"I'll warrant that he will, Nikias."

"I feel very pleasant inside me," Nikias said, and he closed his eyes so that he could blink away another silly tear.

Demetrios got up.

"But now we must look sharp," he said. "Manitza and Papous and the little Penelope, they will be worrying about you. We are going to take you home. Joannes and I have permission to carry you on a stretcher."

"Just—just as if I was wounded," Nikias said, sighing happily.

"I am keeping the best until the last," Demetrios said. He had reached the entrance to the tent and spoke looking back over his shoulder. "Just like the old storyteller I am."

"What do you mean?" Nikias asked.

"The colonel bids me tell you that as brave a deed as yours does not go unrewarded."

"Unrewarded!" Nikias said, not understanding.

"He bade me find out what thing you would like best."

"What thing? But you know what it is: to ride in an aeroplano—and that cannot be."

"About that, I dare not say," Demetrios answered. "A good soldier does not make promises; he leaves that to his officers. I shall tell the colonel what you say. Now, you must have food and then we shall start."

Chapter Twenty-three

IT WAS five days later. Nikias lay on a blanket in front of the fire, with his bandaged shoulder propped against a pillow. Penelope was sitting on a stool beside him, embroidering something. Near her was Thalia hemming a homespun sheet. Manitza was moving about the room, busying herself with the food for supper. Papous was smoking as he lounged in the doorway.

"Did he look well and happy? Did he ask about me?" For the hundredth time Thalia was asking the same questions about Demetrios.

"He looked like a soldier," Nikias said. "But I think he had not forgotten the sheep and you."

Manitza laughed. "Oh, like as not they had men's affairs to talk of, my Thalia," she said. "You are only a woman. See, Nikias, I have baked you your favorite honey cake. You shall have *three* slices."

"Nikias," Penelope said, "this belt I am embroidering, it is for you. It is blue and white like the colors of Greece, and it is very nice, but I will not wait until Christmas to give it to you."

"That is good," said Nikias, contentedly.

"I wish the colonel of your regiment could see it about your waist," Penelope said.

"Silly one," said Nikias. "Why should a great officer have need of seeing me? Girls are very ignorant at times, are they not, Papous?"

"The lad's voice is hoarse," said Manitza in a worried voice. "You are sure you do not feel a chill, Nikias? You were not carrying your potato when you went up the mountain."

Papous winked an eye at Nikias.

"That mountain goat is as well as I am except for a hurt shoulder," he said. "But you women are always making a

169

fuss over ills and herbs and syrups. To my way of thinking, a dose of garlic will cure any sickness except a bad conscience or a broken heart."

Penelope jumped up.

"There are steps coming," she said. "Look, it is Kyr Mihale and Theo."

Nikias could hear Kyr Mihale's hobnailed brogans coming up the path, and Theo's lighter tread behind him. Then he saw the bright red, white, and blue pompons on the brogans and the thick woolen leggings, and Kyr Mihale and Theo were in the room.

"May the good year be with you all," Kyr Mihale said. He sat down on the chest. He looked very important. He cleared his throat.

"What have you in the big wallet at your waist?" asked Papous.

"I have news," said Kyr Mihale and then suddenly he forgot to be proper and act like a schoolteacher. He jumped up, seized Papous around the neck, and swung him off his feet.

"Have you gone mad?" asked Manitza, laughing.

"Papous, Manitza, Nikias—all of you," cried Kyr Mihale. "The sixth regiment—Demetrios' regiment—it has driven back the enemy! It is chasing them beyond the Albanian border!"

"May the holy Virgin be thanked," said Manitza.

"Then—the village is saved!" Papous said in a trembling voice.

"The regiment made a lightning attack," said Kyr Mihale, his eyes shining.

"And to think Nikias did it all," said Penelope.

Thalia laughed excitedly; her cheeks were like roses.

"But of course he did," she cried, "with the aid of Demetrios."

"It is true that Demetrios showed them the pass on which they could cross to outflank the enemy," Kyr Mihale said, "but it was Nikias who warned them of the enemy's presence."

Theo went up to where Nikias was lying.

"Nikias," said Theo, his face red, his voice very hurried, "I am sorry that I laughed at you. You are brave; 'tis I who am the coward."

"Well spoken," said Kyr Mihale. "I think it is our Theo who now shows courage."

"I thank you," Nikias said. He felt embarrassed, and did not look at Theo.

"But good news always comes in double packets," Kyr Mihale said. He was drawing out a long letter with a red seal. He was smiling. He was handing the letter to Nikias. "I have been ordered to give you this," he said.

"For me!" Nikias said, staring at Kyr Mihale. "What can it be? I have never had a letter."

"Best open it and find out," said Papous.

"My—my hand shakes," said Nikias.

"Read it for him, Kyr Mihale," Manitza begged.

171

Kyr Mihale took the envelope and tore it open. He pulled out the sheet of paper inside and began to read:

"My dear Nikias:

"You have done a great, a shining deed for your country. You have saved a Greek regiment. You have shown the courage of Ulysses. It is not in my power to thank you properly. But this one thing I can give you, the thing you asked for: a ride in an aeroplano. On Monday fortnight a messenger in a motorcar will leave here for a city on the coast. He has orders to stop for you in the village, and take you with him. I have little doubt that the good captain of the airport at the place where I shall send you will see to it that my request is granted. You see, he is my kinsman, and besides I have written him of what you did.

"May you always hold the courage you showed that day. I salute you, friend of Greece!

"Aleko Kalamato, Colonel of the Sixth Regiment, Infantry."

Nobody said anything for a minute. You could hear their queer breaths, which seemed to have started and then stuck halfway in their throats. Except for that, it was very, very still in the room. Then Nikias said in a whisper:

"Kyr Mihale, it is not a—joke?"

"No, Nikias," Kyr Mihale answered in a sort of choked-up voice; "it is not a joke."

And then everyone was talking at the same time, laughing, shouting, hugging Nikias, waving the letter. But after a while the noise died down, and Papous said:

"How this war will end is in the hands of God."

"Aye," said Manitza, crossing herself.

"But whether we win or whether we lose," Papous said, "we need not be ashamed of Greece."

"Perseus, Ulysses, all our heroes of old, would say Aye to that," Kyr Mihale said.

"Oh, we shall win," Thalia cried; "we shall win in the end. I feel it—I know it!"

"God grant it!" Manitza said.

"At least," said Kyr Mihale, "we have one small soldier here who is worthy to bear the shield of Perseus."

"If only," cried Theo, his eyes sparkling, "Nikias and I were in that army, we would show them how to fight!"

"For that speech," said Manitza, laughing and giving Theo a little hug, "there must be three slices of honey cake."

Chapter Twenty-four

THE big black car went rushing along the highway. It seemed to Nikias that he had been riding forever. Perhaps that was because so many things had happened that day: the good-bys of Papous and Penelope, Manitza's hug, the tune Kyr Mihale played, the present of a pouch of gunpowder Theo brought, and the new fez with the red tassel that Thalia had made him.

Nikias had not said very much during all the long way they had come. He was a little afraid of the soldier who had a bristling black mustache and frowned as he drove. Nikias supposed he was thinking of battles and didn't want to be disturbed by a boy's talk. They had left the mountain country where the village was, and had come to lowland, to grain fields and olive groves and orchards and little towns. Once they stopped and the soldier and Nikias went into a coffee shop and had bread and cheese and a melon.

Now it was afternoon. The tall cypress trees were beginning to throw thin shadows on the road. Nikias could see the birds flying low.

The soldier said, "You, are you tired?"

"No, master," Nikias said.

"Soon now we will come to the city. Have you ever seen the great sea?"

"No, master."

"Think of that!" said the soldier. "Then you have not laid eyes on the big silver fish or the boats bobbing in the water with their orange sails? You have not felt the *brex* in your face?"

"What is the *brex*?" asked Nikias.

"The afternoon wind from the sea, little ignorant one."

The soldier was smiling. Perhaps he lived in the city, Nikias thought, and so he felt happy to be so close to home. Nikias made up his mind to speak.

"Do you think, master," he said, "that the colonel remembered to tell them in the city that I am coming? He may have been too busy pushing back the enemy."

"Oh," said the soldier, and he smiled again. "The colonel is like a god; he forgets nothing."

"I have never been in a city," said Nikias. "I do not know what one does."

"Well, I do not expect the runners will be exactly out of breath over spreading the news of your arrival," said the soldier, and this time he laughed out loud. "But you need have no worry about *someone's* knowing, I'll warrant you that."

Nikias sat up straighter. He was beginning to feel a queer feeling inside him. He thought it must be because he felt lonely. He must not let the soldier know though. This must be the city. There were houses and a park and big buildings.

Nikias had never seen so many houses in his life. They drove straight on. And after a long time Nikias saw that the car was stopping. They seemed to be in front of a great field. There was a low brick building in front, and it was protected by a high iron fence. Soldiers were marching up and down before the building.

"This is the airport," said the soldier. "We are here."

He slid out of his seat and came around and opened the door on Nikias' side.

"Out you go," he said.

They passed the guard at the gate after the soldier had shown him a piece of paper with a red seal, and they went up the paved walk to the building. There was a room inside where people were waiting. Most of them had uniforms on. The soldier spoke to a young man at a desk, and then they sat down and waited. They waited quite a while. Nikias began to feel even more lonely—if only Demetrios or Paolos were here! Then he cleared his throat angrily. What kind of soldier was he anyway? Had not the colonel said in the letter that he was a soldier of Greece?

And then the man at the desk came over and said something to them, and the soldier smiled at Nikias and said good-by, and then he was gone.

"Come with me," said the young man to Nikias, and they both went through a door into a long hall, and stopped at a second door at the end of the passage. The man knocked very softly and a voice said to come in, and then they were in the room.

It was a big, very long room. There were maps tacked up on the white walls, and pictures of airships, and there were the things called telephones on the desk. A man, in uniform, with gray hair and a stern face was sitting there looking at some papers. Presently he looked up.

"Here is the boy, Nikias Yannio, sir," said the young man.

"Come here," said the officer. Nikias obeyed. "So you are the lad who saved the Sixth Regiment, my cousin's outfit? The heroes of Greece come in small packets these days." Then suddenly he smiled. Nikias thought his face looked just the way a swallow looked when it shook out its wings to fly, all shining and clear. "We have a saying in the air corps," he said, "that a man must earn his right to fly an aeroplano; you, Nikias, have earned yours. Come closer."

Nikias went closer. The officer opened a drawer and took out a little box, opened it, and there, lying on his palm, was a shining pin made in the shape of two silver wings. "See, I pin it on your chest," he said. "Wear it always."

Nikias looked down at the little wings.

"They are—for me?" he said in a whisper.

"For you, Nikias. You see, I have heard what your wish is."

"You—"

"To fly an airship someday."

"Oh," said Nikias.

"We do not every day have little lads who save a regi-

177

ment. You are to have your wish, Nikias; I am going to let you ride in an aeroplano."

"You——" began Nikias. But then he couldn't say any more.

The officer said something to the young man, who went out through another door. The officer looked at his papers. Nikias did not move. Then the door opened again; two people were coming in, the man from the desk and a tall young man in a shining pilot's uniform. Nikias gave a little cry; then he was running across the room right into Paolos' arms.

"Nikias, by all that is good!" said Paolos, and stooped and held him close. Then he quickly straightened and saluted the officer and said, "Your pardon, sir; I forgot myself."

But the man at the desk did not mind; he was smiling again. He did not seem stern at all.

"You two go and forget yourselves some more," he said. "I have given orders, Yannio, for the $R26$ to be warmed up. You should be able in fifteen minutes to show your guest some of the wonders of the port before it grows dark."

Then the officer got up and leaned toward Paolos; he looked just the way Kyr Mihale had the day he brought the news about the victory of the Sixth Regiment.

"I have just heard," he said, "the enemy is falling back all along the line."

"God grant you're right," Paolos said.

Then the officer put his two fingers to his forehead and

Paolos did the same, and then he and Nikias were outside the room. They were walking down a whitewashed passage. They were opening a door. They were outside in the great field—a field full of aeroplanos, and men running about, calling orders. Nikias could hear the thunder of the great motors, could see the great shining wings, the propellers, the painted numbers on the sides of the planos. A young man was speaking to them, showing them the way. They were standing beside an aeroplano. They were putting up a step, and Paolos was walking up it, with Nikias' hand in his.

Paolos was sitting down in a seat in front of a great shining board. There were all sorts of strange knobs and lights on it. Nikias was sitting down beside him. The engines were making a loud sound. Paolos was calling something and then the aeroplano, like a bird, was running, hopping down the field; was slowly rising.

Nikias did not breathe. He thought if he did, he would surely waken. He saw Paolos' hands holding the wheel, pressing the little knobs on the board. And still they were going up.

"Look down," Paolos said. He spoke very loudly to make Nikias hear above the din of the engine.

There was the great blue sea dotted with ships: great steel battleships, smaller steamboats, little sailing boats with colored sails. There was an island covered with crumbling ruins—a second island that looked like a great orchard of leafless trees—a wide river, and winding silver shores. Here and there were people moving about like wooden dolls.

Nikias gave a long sigh. It was exactly as if *he* were flying. He was Perseus going to Atlas' land, the land at the edge of the world. He was Icarus going up, up, to pay a call on the angels. Only there was no wax to melt, no feathers to go tumbling into this blue sea.

"Nikias," Paolos shouted again. He was turning his head; he was smiling at Nikias. "That was pretty swell of the Colonel and Kyr Mihale to fix up this ride for you and me."

"You bet!" Nikias' voice was a whoop that the wind and the roar of the motors both pounced upon.

For a second Paolos did not say anything, then he turned again.

"Know what I'm going to do after this war is over?" he shouted again. "I'm going back home to earn enough money to train you to be the best pilot in Greece. Only I hope you'll always run passenger planes, not warships."

Nikias could only gaze up at Paolos. His heart felt as if it were going to burst.

Paolos reached over and patted Nikias' hand.

"Let's fly," he said.

"Yes!" Nikias shouted back.

That was all Nikias said. He was rubbing one ankle against the other to see whether he really had on winged sandals or not.

"I'm not afraid," he said to himself. "Perseus, do you hear me, I'm not afraid any more!"

181